"What's your game, C.J.?" Chris snarled through clenched teeth.

"Cozy up to the sheriff? Let him think you care, when all the while you're laughing up your sleeve because you've got him hoodwinked?"

"Hoodwinked? Chris, that's not—" The biting coldness of the handcuffs stung C.J.'s wrists as he backed her up against the desk and caged her there, one arm on either side of her shoulders.

"Isn't it? Oh, you tried to get rid of me at first, but once you knew I was interested . . ."

Her chin came up defiantly. "If that's how things look to you—"

"How the hell are they supposed to look? You don't seriously mean to tell me you cared?" She flinched at the harshness of his words, but he plowed on mercilessly. "You used me. And now you figure you'll sweet-talk your way out of jail. Well, it won't work. . . ."

Dear Reader,

Spring is on its way in at last, but we've got some hot books to keep you warm during the last few chilly days. There's our American Hero title, for example: Ann Williams's *Cold, Cold Heart.* Here's a man who has buried all his feelings, all his hopes and dreams, a man whose job it is to rescue missing children—and who can't get over the tragedy of failure. Into his life comes a woman he can't resist, a woman whose child has been stolen from her, and suddenly he's putting it all on the line all over again. He's back to saving children—and back to dreaming of love. Will his cold heart melt? You take a guess!

Mary Anne Wilson completes her "Sister, Sister" duet with *Two Against the World.* For all of you who loved *Two for the Road,* here's the sequel you've been waiting for. And if you missed the first book, don't worry. You can still order a copy—just don't let Ali's story slip through your hands in the meantime!

The rest of the month is filled with both familiar names—like Maura Seger and Amanda Stevens—and new ones—like Diana Whitney, who makes her Intimate Moments debut, and Dani Criss, who's publishing her very first book. I think you'll enjoy everything we have to offer, as well as everything that will be heading your way in months to come. And speaking of the future, look for some real excitement next month, when Intimate Moments celebrates its tenth anniversary with a can't-miss lineup of books, including Patricia Gardner Evans's long-awaited American Hero title, *Quinn Eisley's War.* Come May, Intimate Moments is definitely *the* place to be.

Yours,
Leslie J. Wainger
Senior Editor and Editorial Coordinator

SHERIFF'S LADY

Dani Criss

Silhouette® INTIMATE MOMENTS®

Published by Silhouette Books New York

America's Publisher of Contemporary Romance

SILHOUETTE BOOKS
300 East 42nd St., New York, N.Y. 10017

SHERIFF'S LADY

ISBN: 0-373-07490-5

First Silhouette Books printing April 1993

All the characters in this book have no existence outside the imagination of the author and have no relation whatsoever to anyone bearing the same name or names. They are not even distantly inspired by any individual known or unknown to the author, and all incidents are pure invention.

®: Trademark used under license and registered in the United States Patent and Trademark Office and in other countries.

Printed in the U.S.A.

DANI CRISS

has wanted to write romance since she first read Jane Austen's *Pride and Prejudice*. In high school she dabbled in poetry and short stories, though in her mind, the words *short* and *story* are a contradiction in terms.

She squeezes her writing time between working as an office manager and taking care of her family. She lives in Kansas City with Dan, her wonderful husband of twenty-two years, her two lovely daughters, Crissie and Sara, and a varying assortment of pets.

In loving memory of Sara Mary Curtis, whose loving spirit, spunk and quiet strength I will carry with me always. I love you, Grandma. This one's for you.

Chapter 1

They were running for their lives and their only form of transportation had just quit.

As C. J. Dillon got a whiff of the acrid odor coming from the Toyota's engine, her heartbeat accelerated in panic. Nowhere in her schemes to outmaneuver the men looking for her and Annie was there a provision for car breakdowns on a two-lane back road in northern Wyoming.

"Why are we...*ah-choo*...stopping?" The nasal voice and accompanying sneeze came from Annie, ensconced in the back seat with pillows, blanket, box of tissues and litter bag.

"Something's wrong with the car." C.J. forced a note of calm into her voice, knowing her younger sister would go to pieces if she thought there was anything to worry about. C.J. needed to direct all her thoughts and energy toward solving the present crisis.

"Is it out of gas? Maybe you should have filled up at that station in that so-called town we just passed."

"Redman," C.J. corrected absently as her mind raced to comprehend the situation.

"Whatever. Why you bother to remember the names of these blink-and-you'll-miss-them farm towns is beyond me."

C.J. bothered because minor details that went disregarded usually became major problems. In this case, there was too much at stake to pass anything off as trivial.

Annie's ensuing sneeze was followed by the noise of her blowing her nose once more. Without waiting for the coughing fit that was sure to come next, C.J. stepped out of the car, walked around the front fender and opened the hood. The acrid odor was stronger than it had been from inside.

"Well, damn," she muttered to the September afternoon breeze. In answer, the wind blew the engine's heat back in her face. C.J.'s knowledge of mechanics wasn't extensive, but judging from the heat and the stench coming off the engine, the car's problem would not be a quick fix.

Swallowing the terror that threatened to choke her vocal cords, she stuck her hand through the passenger window. "Hand me some of those tissues."

Annie held up the box so C.J. could pull out as many as she wanted. "What are you going to do?"

"Check the oil." Folding the wad of tissues, C.J. walked back to the engine.

After a few minutes of poking around under the hood, she located the dipstick, pulled it out and frowned at the thick black substance that covered the thin strip of metal. Repeating the procedure she'd seen her Washington, D.C., mechanic perform on her ancient Ford, she wiped the stick across the tissue. Nothing came off.

Her frown deepening, she shoved the stick back into the shaft, pulled it out and wiped it off again. The tissue was dry this time, too. She picked at the black goop on the stick, using her fingernail to pry loose a gooey chunk. She sniffed it, deciding it smelled like hot oil, but the consistency was wrong. Oil was not supposed to solidify.

"C.J...." Annie paused to cough, then stuck her head out the window. "When are we going to get moving?"

"We aren't." C.J. stared at the black stuff on her fingertip as the gravity of the situation soaked in. They weren't going anywhere anytime soon. Her hand shook as she replaced the dipstick. Beads of perspiration dotted her forehead in spite of the cool early-fall air.

"What do you mean, we aren't?"

Just once, C.J. wished she could share her fears with Annie, could lessen this burden she carried alone. But Annie panicked too easily. Striving to project a calm appearance, C.J. walked back to the side of the car.

"Remember the loud noise you heard before we stopped?" she asked cautiously.

Annie shrugged. "You ran over a pop can or something."

"No, the sound came from under the hood. The engine."

"So what do we do now?"

"I don't know."

"Come on. You always know what to do," Annie croaked. "You had three contingency plans on how you would be born, and you've had at least that many for everything that's happened since.''

C.J. sighed. ''This time I'm fresh out.''

The silence was sudden and unbroken, no wind in the trees, no birds chirping, no sound of any kind. Even Annie's sneezing and coughing was momentarily suspended while she absorbed the impact of C.J.'s careless words.

Annie's bright blue eyes widened in her now stark-white face. ''C.J....'' Her voice rose in panic. ''What are we going to do? We can't sit here and wait for Matlock and Jordainne to find us. We don't even have a gun.''

C.J. gripped Annie's narrow shoulders framed by the window and squeezed hard. ''Annie Dillon, you're my sister and I love you dearly, but this is no time to fall apart.''

Her sister's eyes filled with tears. ''I know, I know, but I'm tired and sick and scared. I can't forget that we were meant to die in that car crash.''

C.J. couldn't forget, either. Each time she got behind the wheel she had to fight back the memories of careering down that steep off-ramp toward a busy street in a car without brakes. The men who'd tried to kill them meant business.

C.J. was terrified. More than she had ever been. But admitting that to her sister would create more problems than it would solve. Frequently in times of crisis, the only thing that held Annie together was the belief that C.J. had everything under control.

''I do understand,'' she said placatingly, ''but right now I need to think. Go back to sneezing. I'll figure out something.''

Annie nodded mutely, then her blond head disappeared into the back seat. C.J. waited until the next sneeze came before she walked around to the front of the car where the raised hood hid her from Annie's view.

There was a way out of every predicament, if she just pushed the fear aside long enough to sort through her options. She and Annie could stay where they were and wait for help, but on this deserted back road it might not arrive for hours. Then when someone finally came along, it might be the wrong people—the men hunting them. She and Annie would be sitting ducks.

They had to keep moving, but how far would they get on foot? Should they double back or keep pushing forward? What lay ahead of them? Who was waiting behind them?

So damn many uncertainties. And if she made the wrong choice... She closed her eyes and tried to shake the litany of questions. Her back to the engine, C.J. folded her arms across her chest and eyed the winding road ahead.

No town, not even a farmhouse. Just grass and trees as far as she could see. That's why she'd chosen the back roads—less traffic, less chance of being stopped by a cop, less chance of someone following them unnoticed.

But her strategy complicated the current situation considerably. The only service station she'd seen since crossing the South Dakota-Wyoming border was the one in Redman. A rundown building with one pump in front and a single-bay garage.

Garage... That might or might not mean a mechanic, but there was only one way to find out. C.J.

walked out to the middle of the deserted road and looked down the path they'd traveled. Five minutes at forty miles per hour. How far could they have gotten? Three, maybe four miles. Farther than a Sunday stroll, but not as far as it could have been. At the moment, it was their best option.

She opened her mouth to call to Annie, then stopped as she glimpsed movement in the distance. The words froze in her throat.

Coming down the road toward her was a four-wheel drive vehicle with a light bar on top. Police. Another time she would have welcomed the speedy assistance, but not now.

Police meant connections to data banks all over the country, ultimately to the Federal Task Force on organized crime and FBI Agent Frank Matlock. Was he out looking for them on his own? Or did he have enough clout to issue an APB on the Dillon sisters and drum up charges that would guarantee they'd be detained until he arrived? But instead of taking them to a jail cell, he would escort them to their deaths. She had to assume the worst.

Two stranded motorists, though, C.J. reasoned as the police car slowed, even two females, shouldn't arouse suspicion. As long as she didn't appear overly nervous, the officer shouldn't guess that fear twisted her stomach in a gut-wrenching knot and made her heart pound furiously. Wiping her palms on the legs of her jeans, she watched the Jeep stop across the road from where she stood and worried again about this man's timely appearance. It paid to look for reasons behind coincidence. This time it was critical she question everything.

He seemed in no hurry as he got out and moved toward her with a long, graceful stride, but there was an alertness about him that made her very uncomfortable. His size made her feel even more uneasy. The mere sight of his wide shoulders and muscled biceps would intimidate the most fearsome of men.

Add to that his height, C.J. decided with a touch of alarm as he came closer. She stood five-seven in her running shoes, but her eyes reached only to the sheriff's badge and the nameplate above it. Riker. The name suited him, the consonants strong and hard like his towering physique. Muscles like his—he could be quick as a bobcat, and every bit as powerful. Everything about him could spell trouble. C.J. swallowed hard.

His gaze took in every inch of her, slowly, thoroughly, as if committing each detail to memory. She wanted to squirm under that steady, intent perusal. Heat spilled over her, through her—an odd mixture of alarm and awareness. The latter shouldn't be there, but it was.

"Hello, New York," he said in a deep baritone.

He'd read the license plates on the car, C.J. realized uneasily. So much the better if he believed they were from New York, as long as he hadn't run a make on the stolen tags. Would he have had time to do that?

She forced what she hoped was a casual smile. His eyes were as green as the grassy landscape and the needles on the straight pine trees. They glided over her frame once again, but she couldn't read any hostility in them, or in his easy stance. He just seemed curious, in a very male sort of way.

What should she make of that? And of the electric tingle that traveled up her spine in reaction to his obvious interest?

"Hello, Wyoming. Is your timing always this good?" she asked guardedly.

"I try not to keep a damsel in distress waiting."

The warmth and friendliness in his rich resonant voice made C.J. want to relax, to forget fears and strategies and give herself up to the playful breeze and the powerful, commanding presence of the man standing in front of her. He was safety and friendliness, but, she forcibly reminded herself, the men who had tried to kill her and her sister had seemed friendly and safe, too, at first. Her wariness returned with a jolt.

From the car window came a sneeze followed by a raspy voice. "C.J., have you figured out what…oh."

Without turning around C.J. knew Annie had spotted the lawman and was now scrambling around the car's back seat in search of a comb to tame her tousled blond curls and a compact to powder her red nose.

"Appears I should make that 'damsels.'" Riker's eyes glittered with amusement. "What's wrong with your car?"

He seemed more inclined to assist than arrest, C.J. decided, walking toward the Toyota. She hoped she was reading him right. She preferred to handle her problems alone, but this one was way out of her league. She needed help and this handsome and very virile sheriff was the only one offering it. Those shoulders of his looked strong enough to withstand any assault, strong enough to bear a thousand burdens and then some.

"I'm not sure," she said, reining in her unsettling, runaway awareness of this man. "First there was this horrible stench, then the oil light in the dash came on, then the engine quit. The oil seems awfully thick."

"Thick?" Under the brim of his hat, one dark brown brow rose.

C.J. pulled out the dipstick, scraped off a chunk of the black goop and showed it to him.

"That's the oil?" His low, drawn-out whistle didn't convey the encouragement she had hoped for.

"Do you think a couple of fresh quarts would fix it?"

"Nope."

The sound of finality, she thought, muttering a curse. Under any other circumstances, she would never have bought a car without having a mechanic check it out. But cash had been in short supply and time critical. Their lives had depended on getting far away fast, and in a vehicle that couldn't be traced to her or her sister. She'd abandoned her Ford in New York, bought the Toyota from a man there and prayed it would make it to Seattle with a lot of detours to throw Matlock off their trail. Against her cautious instincts, she'd taken a chance on the car, a calculated risk. And now she was paying the price.

"Can you fix it?" Annie, her hair freshly combed and makeup reapplied, stood beside Riker.

"Afraid not," he answered, glancing down at her.

"Then what can we do?" She dabbed at her nose and raised her pleading blue eyes to the lawman's face.

At twenty, she still had an air of innocence and vulnerability few people could resist. Even C.J. wasn't immune to it. But Riker only gave Annie an indulgent smile, then turned back to C.J.

"I have a tow bar on the back of the Jeep," he told her. "I can pull you to Mike's garage in Redman."

"Oh, that would be wonderful, wouldn't it, C.J.?"

C.J.'s relief was tempered with a lot of caution. "I wouldn't want to take you out of your way. If you could just radio for a tow..."

Chris considered the woman in front of him through a narrowed gaze, surprised by her resistance to his help, by her stiff posture and the intensity of her fascinating blue-gray eyes. The only thing relaxed about her was the long chestnut curls the wind had blown into casual chaos—an interesting contrast to her sober and controlled composure.

His attention had zeroed in on her from his first glimpse of her long slender frame. The closer he'd gotten, the more he'd liked the view. He'd found himself hoping her car's problem might keep her in these parts for a day or two. The lady, though, clearly was not interested in his flirtations. Still, she ought to at least be grateful he'd come along when he did.

"No trouble," Chris told her. "I have business in Redman, anyway."

He wondered if she was this wary with everyone she met. From the looks of the oil on the dipstick, he might have that day or two he wanted with her. He was interested enough to make the effort to get past her wariness, but would his determination be enough with this woman?

"Don't mind C.J. She always looks a gift horse in the mouth. Ex...cuse me." The blonde turned as the sneeze she'd tried to stifle escaped.

So the lady's name was C.J., and she *was* extremely cautious by nature. Chris realized he would have his work cut out, but it would be worth it to see her smile, he'd bet. He could imagine how an all-out grin would light her eyes. That image strengthened his resolve.

"I'll back the Jeep up to the car and get you hooked up." With another warm smile he headed back to his vehicle.

Standing beside Annie, C.J. watched him maneuver the Jeep into position. There was a dreamy expression on her sister's pixie face.

"Isn't he gorgeous?" Annie said.

C.J. didn't answer, hoping to discourage her sister's curiosity. This was not the time for a casual flirtation.

"Don't tell me that photographer's eye of yours didn't notice his smile," Annie persisted.

"I had other things on my mind." C.J. had noticed, though, and in spite of the danger following them, despite the potential threat this man represented, she'd been intrigued. That realization puzzled and startled her.

"Well, this is a first," Annie continued. "An interesting face and you aren't running for your camera. I wonder how he got that little crook in his nose."

Through her fears, the remark piqued C.J.'s curiosity even more. As Riker walked back to the Toyota, she stared at the barely noticeable crook that marred the straight, wide ridge of his nose. The result of a fight, most likely. He was the take-no-guff type, she'd bet. He had that air of one who gave orders, but didn't take them, one who wouldn't run from trouble, one who would get things done. Probably by the book, she added grimly.

He handed her his hat, then ducked under the little car to hook the cables to the undercarriage. That done, he stood beside her, brushing off the dust that clung to his brown uniform pants and shirt. The action drew C.J.'s eyes to the entrancing width of his shoulders again, then to the play of muscles across his back and to his trim hips and thighs outlined in the fitted trousers. She could admire his well-developed form for a very long time, could get lost in photographing it from different angles.

He held out a hand and she automatically returned his hat. When he didn't place it back on his head, she took the opportunity to study his hair. The color of dark chocolate, just a shade away from black, with a hint of curl to the short thick strands. Though the curl didn't detract from his masculinity, it did soften the overall ruggedness—made his jaw appear less square, his jade-green eyes less intimidating, his size less overwhelming.

Still, he was more than six feet of solid muscle and carefully controlled strength. Between that and the intelligence in his eyes, he would make a formidable foe. C.J. knew with startling certainty that were he the one chasing them, she and Annie wouldn't stand a chance. She shivered and pulled her jean jacket close.

"Cools off early this time of year," he commented. "If you stay in these parts, you'll need heavier gear."

Was he fishing for information? C.J. couldn't tell. The remark was casual enough and his pleasant expression gave nothing away. However...

"Thanks for the advice," she said coolly.

He frowned, then nodded. "Hop in and we'll head for the garage."

C.J. turned and saw Annie already situated in the Jeep's front seat, her slender legs stretched out in front of her and a box of tissues on her lap. Riker opened the side door and let C.J. in the back seat.

"We don't get many tourists driving through here," he said once they were on the road. "Especially from halfway across the country. Where were you headed?"

"Billings," Annie answered without hesitation.

Behind her, C.J. tensed at the sheriff's question, knowing others were sure to follow. Annie had never been able to keep secrets, and even though her sister realized the gravity of their present situation, C.J. still feared Annie would slip and say more than she should.

This particular stranger had an innate curiosity concerning anything out of the ordinary—like two women traveling the Wyoming back roads. He was also a cop, with connections that could spell disaster for them.

"Interstate 90 takes you right there." The sheriff glanced over his shoulder at C.J. "On this road, you'll have to double back thirty miles or so once you get into Montana."

She nodded. "I know."

"C.J. thinks the back roads are more scenic," Annie told him.

C.J. breathed in relief, glad Annie had followed their well-rehearsed script. Scenery was the only plausible explanation certain to allay this lawman's suspicions. C.J. didn't want Sheriff Riker any more interested in them than he already was.

"That's true," he agreed. "Are you visiting family in Billings?"

"There's just me and C.J.," Annie chattered on. "I'm Annie. That's my sister, C.J."

C.J. relaxed a little, grateful that her long lectures on exercising caution seemed to have done some good.

Annie hadn't given the sheriff their surname. That would be disastrous should he decide to run a check on them. Once he discovered she and Annie were wanted, they would be doomed. Now if only she could get Annie to be less talkative.

"Chris Riker," he said, wondering at the way C.J. stared daggers at her younger sister's back. She was certainly an enigma, he thought as they neared Redman. A puzzle he would enjoy solving, he thought as Annie started coughing again. "Your cold sounds really bad. Have you seen a doctor?"

"Hasn't been . . . time . . ."

C.J. quickly squeezed Annie's shoulder as the coughing started again. "Be quiet," she said in a firm tone that indicated she was accustomed to being obeyed. "The less you talk, the less you'll cough."

They rode the last mile in silence broken only by Annie's cough and frequent sneezes. Chris made a mental note to load up on orange juice for the next few days so he didn't catch her cold.

Though he sympathized with the kid, it was C.J. who captured his attention and activated his imagination. She had about nine years on Annie, but the age difference was more apparent in manner than looks. C.J. was as attractive as her sister, but in a different way. Where the kid was a classic beauty, C.J.'s good looks were more subtle, yet far more interesting. Especially her determined chin and fascinating eyes. Instead of washing out the bright blue color, the steely gray brightened the expressive depths.

"Mike's not very talkative, but he's a first-rate mechanic," Chris told them as he pulled up to the station to let his two passengers out at the door.

No one would guess Mike's talent from the run-down station, C.J. thought, eyeing the waiting room. She settled Annie on the greasy chair, figuring it was more stable than the black vinyl couch that was minus one leg and most of its cottony stuffing.

While Riker and the mechanic backed the Toyota into the single bay, C.J. gave her attention to her sister. Annie's pale cheeks were dotted with two bright spots of red. Her fever was undoubtedly up and her one burst of energy when Riker arrived on the scene was gone. C.J. dropped two quarters into the pop machine, careful to touch only the tip of her finger to the grease-coated selection button. She wiped her finger on her jeans, handed Annie the can, then leaned against the doorway looking out on the quiet town.

There were a handful of frame structures built side by side. Feed store, barber shop, grocery store. Across the street was a two-story building with a dilapidated sign in front that said Hotel-Restaurant in sun-bleached blue paint.

Main Street was deserted. No other cars, none of the hectic activity that marked the major cities she'd lived in, not even the slower-paced goings-on of the Nebraska town she and Annie had grown up in—no retired couples taking an afternoon walk, no young mothers pushing baby strollers, no kids playing.

She and Annie needed to be moving. Though C.J. hadn't spotted anyone following them, she had no way of knowing whether she'd thrown Matlock off their trail, or whether he was only two steps behind them, waiting to finish the deed he'd botched when he'd cut the brake lines on her car.

She paced to the doorway of the work area. The stocky mechanic came out from under the car and said a few words to Riker, who just shook his head. C.J. walked over to the two men, still unaccountably aware of the sheriff's size and obvious strength. She would give anything to know that she could trust him enough to tell him what she and Annie were running from. It would be so good to put this fear into the hands of a pro. But he knew nothing about her. As a lawman, he would take Matlock's word over hers in a minute.

"That's all the oil that was in the drip pan." Mike poked at the few black flakes in the pan he held.

Riker gave a long, drawn-out whistle, the same as he'd done at the glimpse of the car's dipstick.

"So how bad is it?" C.J. braced herself, certain she wouldn't like the answer.

"You wanna tell her?" Mike asked, his Native American features classically stoic.

Riker looked from her to the pan and back, then shook his head. "Nope. I'm going to gas up the Jeep."

Mike gave a disgusted grunt as Riker walked out the door. When it was apparent he wasn't coming back, Mike turned to C.J. "Know anything about cars?"

When she shook her head, he launched into a description of an engine's workings—head gaskets, valves, blocks and other terminology she'd heard of but knew nothing about. He must have noticed her confusion, because eventually he stopped in mid-sentence and gave another disgusted grunt.

"You ruined the engine letting it run out of oil." He set the pan on the worktable. "When you stopped for gas didn't anybody offer to check under the hood?"

"Yes, but I was always in a hurry."

"Seems you ain't in such a hurry now."

C.J. counted to ten, knowing she'd gain nothing by losing her temper, or letting fear overwhelm her. Besides, Mike was right. She'd let haste, and fear, make her careless.

"How soon can you have it fixed?" she asked.

"Needs a new engine. Findin' one around here won't be easy." He glanced at the rusty red Toyota and grunted again. "Best get another car."

"Would anyone around here have one for sale?"

"Not that I know. All of us hang on to our autos. Have to. Closest place to look is Casper."

C.J. followed him over to the sink, thinking. She didn't like either option he'd offered, but they were her only choices. Making the wrong one could have disastrous consequences.

A new car? She chewed her lower lip. She hadn't registered the Toyota after buying it in New York because the paperwork would have clued Matlock in on what she was driving. He would have put the car's description and license number in the APB. Driving a car with no tags would have been even riskier. Some cop would notice the absent license plate, stop her and probably arrest her when he discovered the car wasn't registered to her. Though it had gone against the grain, her only alternative had been to steal plates off a car in a mall parking lot in upstate New York.

Could she get by with putting the stolen plates on another car? It appeared she would have to buy from a dealer instead an individual. If that was the case, she wouldn't be able to dodge the paperwork. Then, too, what guarantee did she have that a second used car would be any more reliable than the first?

There was the financial aspect to consider, as well. She'd paid for all their expenses from the cash she'd hurriedly withdrawn from her bank account before leaving D.C., knowing that using a credit card would make it child's play for Matlock to track them down. After nearly two weeks on the road, their funds were running very low.

A new engine wouldn't be much cheaper, and though the car wasn't worth the investment, the repairs wouldn't involve any paperwork that might give Matlock a line on them.

"How soon before you know if you can get an engine?" she asked.

"Have to call around, see if there's one to be had. Then a couple days maybe to get it here."

"And to put it in?"

"Day or two. If there ain't no problem." The phone rang. Mike turned to answer it, leaving C.J. with her thoughts.

Three days minimum, probably longer. Was it safe to stay put for that long? They could use the rest. Sounds of Annie's coughing carried in from the other room. She needed time to recuperate, and C.J. herself could use a break. Her nerves were stretched to the limit. Still, she wouldn't be able to relax until she made it to Seattle, to Keith Taylor and the protection her journalist friend offered.

She looked out onto the main street again. Other than Riker at the gas pump, there was no activity. Who would think to look for two female fugitives in a town this small and quiet? Who would even know the town was here unless they stumbled on to it? That was a definite advantage. It appeared replacing the engine would be the less risky option.

She hadn't gotten wind of the FBI agent following her. For now, she would have to gamble that she'd lost him. As long as Sheriff Riker didn't run a make on those stolen plates, she and Annie should be safe for a while.

She turned to Mike as he hung up the phone. "Let's try for the engine first."

Though his face remained impassive, she had the feeling he wanted to comment on the wisdom of throwing good money after bad. But he only nodded, then walked over to the cash register.

Riker paid for the gas, pocketed the change and the receipt, then turned to C.J. "You'll be without transportation for a while, I take it. There's a chain motel in Northfield."

"What about the one across the street? Is it open for business?" she asked, hoping it wasn't as deserted as the outside made it appear. She preferred to be close by in case someone came nosing around the car. Even a split-second warning was better than being taken by complete surprise. And the minute the car was ready, she wanted to be back on the road.

Riker nodded. "The only business Shari's had in a long time has been at the diner, but I imagine she can put you up if you're sure you want to stay in Redman. Northfield's got a few craft shops to wander through, a grocery and drugstore, even a movie theater. And my office is there. I can drive you back here when your car is ready. Maybe take you sight-seeing, since you'll be here a few days."

C.J. didn't like the sound of that. She had no doubt the sheriff would be a wonderful and exciting escort. Under any other circumstances she would jump at the chance to spend time with him, get to know him. But that was too dangerous now.

"I don't want shops and sight-seeing, and I don't want to drive any more," Annie said. "Let's try the hotel across the street, C.J., please?"

One look at Annie's overbright eyes, red nose and too-pale face was enough to convince C.J. her sister needed a rest. She tossed the empty pop can into the trash. "Let me get something out of the car."

She opened the passenger door, reached in the floor of the front seat and pulled out a big canvas bag. She would come back for their suitcase once she had Annie settled and Riker was gone. The fact that two women were traveling cross-country with only one suitcase might look suspicious to him. But they hadn't dared to go back to their apartment for their things. The suitcase and the few clothes in it had been acquired on the road.

"That looks heavy." Riker reached for the bag.

His long fingers looked strong and very capable. C.J. found herself wanting to hand him the bag and all her problems with it. The alarming feeling made her withdraw.

"I can manage." With a weary feeling, she slung the wide strap over her shoulder and headed for the door. The sooner the sheriff went back to his business, whatever that was, the better for her runaway senses. Just his towering over her sent her pulse racing erratically. She couldn't afford this unusually strong attraction, or the unsettling urge to lean on him. Not now.

"My sister never goes anywhere without every piece of camera equipment she owns," Annie informed him solemnly, "and she never trusts anyone else to carry it."

The bag's safety was more important than ever, C.J. thought. Tucked under the bottom lining were the documents that would put Sen. Alex Jordainne and FBI Agent Frank Matlock permanently out of business.

"Won't people think it odd when we arrive with a police escort?" she mused dryly as they approached the hotel door.

Riker smiled, kind of a crooked half smile, C.J. thought, catching another glimpse of that pure male vitality Annie must have noticed earlier.

"I'll tell Shari it's a rescue mission," he said, "and that she should call me if you give her any trouble."

"She won't have any trouble from me." Annie pulled another tissue out of the nearly empty box. "I'm going to sleep for a week."

"You'll have the place to yourselves. Since the interstate opened, Redman rarely has anyone even passing through."

That comment made C.J. feel better about holing up for a few days. She got Annie upstairs to their room and watched her drop gratefully onto one twin bed. After stashing the camera bag under the other, C.J. went back down to get their suitcase from the car. Chris Riker was waiting at the foot of the stairs.

"Thanks for your help," she said as they walked back to the garage, hoping against hope he would take the hint and leave. He was entirely too interested. And interesting.

"It's been a very pleasant diversion."

His voice held that warmth again. It beckoned to her senses, awakened them at a time when she couldn't afford the complication. She looked up and found him grinning. He had an arresting smile, she thought, then groaned to herself over the unintentional pun.

"Low crime rate in these parts, Sheriff?"

"As a rule. But we find enough work to keep us earning our pay."

"Such as rescuing stranded motorists?"

"Yeah. Usually it's in the middle of a winter storm, though." He pulled open the station door, held it for her, then, to her dismay, followed her inside.

Standing in the doorway to the work area, Chris watched her speak to Mike, then walk over to the car's trunk. The job of rescuing had its perks, he thought as she bent to set a suitcase on the floor. Her tight jeans emphasized her long slender legs and nicely rounded bottom. Looking at that derriere, no jury in the world would convict him for the wayward direction his thoughts took.

And they were wayward, indeed. He'd known her for less than an hour and already he was imagining what it would feel like to hold her against him, to kiss her thoroughly. His thoughts about a woman had never progressed so far so fast.

Chris caught Mike grinning at him and decided he'd leered long enough. When she shut the car trunk, he decided he wasn't in any hurry to say goodbye to this lady.

"Let me help you." He picked up the oversize suitcase. "Is this all? You and your sister travel lighter than most women, don't you?"

C.J.'s stomach muscles tightened. "You shouldn't stereotype, Sheriff. I can manage that." She frowned when he didn't put the case down. Either her earlier hint was too subtle, or he had a reason for sticking close to her. That thought made her stomach tighten even more. "This is above and beyond the call of duty, isn't it?"

She was very cautious, and Chris sensed she wasn't accustomed to accepting assistance. An independent lady. He didn't know why that bothered him, especially when most of the women from these parts were, by necessity, self-sufficient and he didn't mind that. But with C.J. he did. He headed for the door before she could object further.

"Anxious to get rid of me?" He locked his gaze with hers.

"No, but..."

"Good, because in Wyoming we rescuers are hard to shake. In fact..." He paused to shoulder the station door open. "We always stick around for our reward."

"Reward?" she asked, her eyes narrowed warily.

"Company for dinner tonight, you and your sister," he added, hoping if Annie were included C.J. would be more inclined to accept the invitation.

She didn't answer, didn't look up at him as they crossed the street, but her shoulders were stiff. He opened the hotel door and carried the suitcase inside, putting it on the floor when she stopped at the foot of the stairs and turned toward him. Her chin was set at a determined angle.

"I can manage from here," she said in the firm tone she'd used with her sister.

"What about dinner?" Chris pressed.

From upstairs came the muffled sounds of Annie sneezing and coughing. C.J. glanced toward their room door and shook her head. "Not tonight. Annie and I are too tired."

Chris knew when to back off. No matter how enticing the woman, he wasn't one to butt his head against a brick wall. However, he'd never been able to resist the challenge of finding a way around, or over, one. Unless he missed his guess, that suitcase he'd carried in was full of clothes, not food. And the hotel dining room was the only restaurant in town. He whistled as he walked back to the Jeep.

Keith Taylor answered the pay phone on the first ring. "You're late."

"I know. I'm sorry," C.J. told him.

"Standing in the damp chill in one of Seattle's less attractive districts isn't a wise idea." He sighed. "But I had to know you were still safe."

"Thanks," C.J. said, grateful for her friend's caring. "It's Annie..."

"What's wrong with her?" Keith asked anxiously. "She's not chickening out now, is she? It's too late—"

"She won't chicken out. I was playing nursemaid. She's got a horrible cold. If she gets worse..."

"She'll be all right. You've got to quit anticipating problems."

"Like you?"

He was as cautious as she, C.J. knew, always looking over his shoulder. Occupational hazard, he'd told her that first assignment they worked on three years ago. Survival instinct, she'd countered. Both were true. That's why he'd arranged to receive her calls at odd times and at various pay phones he'd long ago scoped out, just in case his home or office phones had been tapped. He frequently investigated people with a lot of pull, people who would take any precaution necessary, including tapping his phones, to keep from being exposed.

"Keith, the car quit," she said quietly.

He swore. "When?" he asked.

"Yesterday afternoon. The engine's shot."

"Damn! Have you seen any sign of our men before or since?"

"None. But that doesn't mean they're not somewhere close by."

As she gave Keith more details on her situation, he cursed again. They hadn't counted on this complication—C.J. and her sister trapped somewhere without transportation, without help.

"The town's so small it doesn't even rate a dot on the map," she finished.

"Then that should work to your advantage," he said. "You're doing all you can for now. Quit worrying and leave everything else to me."

"How's the background check on Jennings going so far?"

"Too early to tell," he answered quickly. "It may be next week before I have anything solid on him."

"That long?" She wanted to know now whether it was safe to turn over the papers she had to Seattle's FBI head, or whether he was a cop on the take, too. "Keith, I don't know if I can stand the strain that long."

"Jennings is fairly new in town, Flash, and a thorough investigation takes time. You won't have transportation for three or four days, anyway."

She sighed wearily. "No, but I have a very inquisitive sheriff hanging around."

"Do you think he's on to you?" Keith asked, his voice laced with alarm.

"I don't know. He just seems . . . interested. You know. He tried to get me to have dinner with him."

Keith chuckled softly.

"This is hardly a laughing matter," she scolded.

"You're right. It's just that I've never known anyone who worked so hard to avoid relationships. This sheriff's interest in you would be funny if the situation weren't so serious."

"That's easy for you to say. You don't have to be on guard every moment, watching every word . . . I'm stretched to the breaking point."

"Just be your normal evasive self and you'll do fine," Keith assured her. "You've got the number where you can reach me in the morning?"

"Yeah, and the time."

"Okay. I'll see what I can do to step things up."

He wouldn't let her down, she thought, hanging up. Last week she'd called him from a pay phone in West Virginia, asking for his help. She had evidence that would prove the country's best-liked senator and an FBI agent were working for people engaged in nearly a dozen illegal activities. And Matlock had tried to kill her and her sister.

They knew Matlock wasn't the only FBI man on the take. That's why they'd decided it would be best for C.J. to go it alone rather than try to enlist the help of a cop she didn't know, to keep moving long enough to give Keith time to check out Jennings.

She and Annie weren't going anywhere until their car was repaired, but how long did they have before Matlock caught up with them?

Chapter 2

While Annie slept in their room upstairs, C.J. sat in the hotel diner, pushing a bite of apple pie around on her plate. The pie, as well as the bowl of stew she'd eaten, tasted great, but she couldn't summon much enthusiasm for food. Her thoughts kept running to Chris Riker, to her startling awareness of him. It had been a long time since a man had attracted her so thoroughly, and even longer since she'd trusted one enough to let him get close to her.

She wouldn't let the sheriff get that close, either, but she didn't know what to make of her reaction to him. She'd wanted to accept his invitation to dinner tonight, but the danger involved forced her to hold back. He was already curious about her, and though she'd sensed his interest was personal rather than professional, that didn't make being with him any safer. One question usually led to another and sooner or later her evasive replies would wear thin. She would be well advised to stay as far away from him as possible, regardless of how much she longed to explore this attraction to him.

With a sigh, she turned her thoughts to Keith Taylor. He was the only person she'd contacted since she'd started running. She had to be certain the person she went to for help wasn't connected with FBI Agent Matlock, or Senator Jordainne, or the criminals backing them. But she hadn't known where to turn, or even how to check into someone's background. Then she'd thought of Keith.

Three years ago they'd worked together for a Seattle newspaper, he a tough journalist making a name exposing corrupt politicians and police officials, and she the photographer who documented his claims on file. Keith had never taken a bribe or killed an investigation, not even when threatened. He was one of the few people she trusted with her life.

She only hoped he would find out soon if this Hal Jennings was an honest cop. Where would she go if it turned out he was working for the same people who had Jordainne and Matlock on their payroll?

At the sound of footsteps, C.J. tensed, then glanced up to examine the newcomers to the nearly empty dining room. Two men in worn jeans, denim jackets and battered Stetsons. Locals, she realized when the waitress addressed them by name and led them over to one of the booths.

The diner, as immaculate as the hotel and just as sparsely furnished, did boast a jukebox. The shorter of the two men dropped some change in and made his selections. In a moment the strains of a country-and-western ballad filled the small room. The elderly couple at a nearby table nodded as though the song was a favorite. At one of the booths a child in a booster chair clapped his hands, laughing when his parents smiled. C.J. felt some of her tension ebb away, only to feel it return as Chris Riker's tall frame appeared next to the chair opposite hers.

She froze, scrutinizing his expression for any sign of aggressiveness or hostility. All she found was purely male interest. Then she noticed he wasn't in uniform.

The other activity in the diner faded into barely audible background noise. All her senses jerked to full attention, focusing on the aura of sexuality he exuded so effortlessly. She felt drawn to him, aware that her resistance was only halfhearted at best.

His jeans rode low on his hips and molded suggestively to his firm thighs. The sleeves of his white shirt were rolled up to his elbows. She could imagine running her fingers through the dark hair that covered his muscular forearms, feeling the power and warmth under her hands.

He looked every bit as formidable as he did in uniform, and as appealing. Power and passion. She would do well to forget his sex appeal, she admonished herself. His intrusion should annoy her, be more unwelcome. Very unwelcome, in fact. This wasn't the time to be considering a flirtation. No matter how handsome and charming he was, he had access to police computers across the country.

He eased into the chair. Her spine stiffened at the shock wave of awareness when she felt the warmth of his thigh next to hers under the small table.

"I'm glad I didn't miss you," he said. "I'd planned to be here sooner, but I had some last-minute things to take care of at the office."

She frowned. Her heartbeat skipped. What type of last-minute things, she wanted to demand, then decided he wasn't there to arrest her when he flashed her one of his irritatingly devastating grins. A grin she should be immune to, she thought furiously, and nervously. Why weren't her hormones responding to reason?

"You don't take no for an answer, do you?" she asked, offering no apology for her bluntness.

"Nope. I'm very persistent when there's something I want." He turned his killer smile on the waitress standing beside the table. "Hi, Tammy."

"Sheriff. Glad you stopped by. I wanted to thank you for that talk you gave my boy."

"I wasn't sure how you'd take it—my agreeing that there were more possibilities for him outside Redman and all."

"It is hard to hear Jake talk of leaving." She sighed. "But there's nothing for him here, and he would just go back to boozing with his pals and getting into trouble."

"Jake's got a good head on his shoulders. When I picked him up, he'd already figured out he didn't want to spend the rest of his life staring into the bottom of a bottle."

"Well, getting that advice from you didn't hurt any." She glanced at C.J. "We think a lot of our sheriff. We just hope he won't decide to go back to the big city."

"I stay where I'm appreciated." Chris leaned back in his chair, relaxed and obviously determined to stay. "And where I'm fed. What's on the menu tonight?"

Tammy took a pencil and order pad from her pocket. "Meat loaf, fried chicken or beef stew."

"Meat loaf. Ask Shari if I can sit in next time she makes it. I followed her recipe to the letter, but mine still didn't come out near as good as hers."

"It's her special touch makes the difference. Apple pie, too?"

"Yeah. Thanks." He waited until Tammy had filled his coffee cup and left, then grinned at C.J. again. "I warned you we rescuers were hard to shake."

"Sounds as if I'm not the only one you've rescued lately." Against her better judgment she'd been intrigued by his conversation with Tammy, by the fact that he was liked and respected by the people in these parts.

He shrugged nonchalantly. "Jake just turned seventeen and is trying to decide what to do with himself. Mostly all I did was listen. You and your sister have been my only real rescue since the blizzard last April."

"And now you've gotten your reward."

He smiled again. "The deal was for two dinner companions. Your sister didn't feel up to coming down?"

C.J. shook her head. "She's sound asleep. She's hardly even coughed."

"The rest will do her good." He stared thoughtfully into his coffee cup for a moment, then looked up, his expression sober. "Since you'll be stationary for a few days, you might want to have a doctor look at her."

He was right about that, she thought. It would be a tremendous relief to know for sure that Annie would be all right. "Is there one in town?"

"Northfield, but Doc's out making calls this week." Chris looked down at the fork in her right hand and raised an eyebrow. "Shouldn't play with your food, especially something as tasty as Shari's pie."

C.J. flashed him a saccharine smile, then glanced at the pie she'd been pushing around on the plate. She popped the bite into her mouth. "Better?"

"The smile certainly is." Even though it lacked genuineness, it had made her eyes brighten for a brief moment, and the corners of her mouth turn up. She'd looked very tempting. "That's the first one I've seen from you."

"Yes, well, sick sisters and car breakdowns provide more tension than entertainment."

"Agreed, but you've got the car situation under control, and as far as your sister goes..." He took out a business card, printed a phone number on the back in neat block letters, then passed the card to C.J. "That's my home number. Call me there if she gets worse during the night and you decide Doc should look at her. He's at the reservation clinic right now, but I can radio him and get him back in a hurry."

She pushed another bite of pie around on the plate while Tammy brought his order and refilled his coffee. His offer of assistance made C.J. leery. Why was he so interested in her welfare, or Annie's?

He was one magnificent male specimen, and under normal circumstances C.J. might have been intrigued by his interest, if that's all it was. But she had too much on her mind now. She didn't have the patience to entertain a lonesome country sheriff, regardless of what being with him did to her suddenly awakened hormones.

"Do you go this far out of your way for everyone, or am I receiving preferential treatment?" she asked once the waitress walked away.

Chris took a moment to sample the meat loaf and mashed potatoes, then looked up from the plate. Her chin jutted out defiantly. All because he was going out of his way to be helpful and pleasant. Certainly nothing to raise anyone's hackles. She was definitely on the defensive, and for no apparent reason. He had the feeling more was going on with her and her sister than auto troubles and a delay in their itinerary.

"Why does it bother you that you might have to accept help?" he asked. "None of us are so independent that we can't use a helping hand every now and then."

C.J. set her fork down and pushed the plate aside. He'd picked up on the fact that she preferred to take care of things on her own. The man's insight was unsettling. What else about her had he picked up?

If only she knew whether she could trust him. But she'd trusted a lawman before and had barely escaped being killed. She had no definite idea how far Matlock's contacts reached. This was not the time to take chances, no matter how badly she longed to share her fears with someone. With Chris Riker.

"You're licensed to practice tableside psychoanalysis, I take it," she said, her body tensed. Better she discourage this man now, though she doubted that would be easy.

"I took some psychology courses through the police academy, but it doesn't take a degree to recognize resentment. So what's your problem with my offer of help?" Watching her intently, he took another bite of meat loaf.

"Maybe it's personal." C.J. fixed him with an icy stare, a look she used to cool a guy's ardor when he got overly interested.

He considered her words, chewing slowly. Finally he swallowed and shook his head. "Nope. Can't be. I'm as likable as they come."

She heard the ego in his words and the teasing laughter behind them. Surprised by his humor, she laughed softly and, in spite of her fears, found most of her annoyance evaporating.

He'd been generous with his time and assistance, solicitous over Annie's health, and as he pointed out, he was a hard man to dislike. In fact, her problem wasn't with him at all. His self-confidence and assurance were relaxing; his air of capability, comforting and calming. Her problem was with his occupation. She had learned firsthand that men sworn to uphold the law wielded a lot of power, and not all of them were honest.

She looked into his dark green eyes, feeling their warmth reach out to her. She drew a deep breath to steady her stumbling heartbeat. She could truly come to enjoy being with him. If only it wasn't the wrong time. "Sorry if I was . . ."

"Rude?" he supplied with his alluring smile.

"Brusque," she corrected.

"As in ungracious, taciturn—"

"As in I deserved that, but accept my apology or I'll withdraw it." She tried to sound miffed that he was returning the hard time she'd given him, but she couldn't quite carry it off when he grinned so appealingly. Could anyone stay angry with him for long?

"Accepted." He set his fork down and reached for his coffee cup. "All kidding aside, I realize you're wise to be cautious, two women traveling alone, especially through these rural towns where you don't know anyone. . . ."

He let his words trail off suggestively, but C.J. chose to ignore his unspoken question. He was fishing for information again, she sensed. But she couldn't tell him why she and Annie were there, so it was better to say nothing. Besides, he was a much more interesting subject.

He was just a few years away from forty, she guessed, studying the few strands of silver streaking through his dark hair. She liked the way the lines at the corners of his eyes and the brackets around his mouth deepened when he smiled. And she'd enjoyed the challenge of matching wits with him. She'd spent too much time around Annie lately, she thought wryly.

"How'd you end up driving through this part of Wyoming?" he asked, his curiosity changing directions for the moment.

C.J. tensed again. The man was extremely persistent. This question was no more than a paraphrasing of his earlier ones. He wasn't going to let her dodge him for long.

"My father was a history teacher." She smiled at those memories. For all his exasperating quirks and foibles, Andrew Dillon had been a loving, gentle man. A man who had tended to trust too easily. Her smile faded. "He always talked about Wild Bill, Calamity Jane, Buffalo Bill. Annie and I wanted to see some of the country they lived in," she finished, hoping this lie would add credence to the reason Annie had given for their traveling the back roads instead of the interstate.

"Sounds as if he really liked the Old West era."

"It was his passion. Our house was full of antiques and memorabilia. Especially books. He could tell you facts about anything that happened in the 1800s—bi-

ographies, life-styles, economic conditions west of the
Mississippi.''

"Did your mother share his passion?"

"She was more amused by it than anything. Except
when it came to dusting the memorabilia."

His laughter was warm and rich, as if it came easy
and often. It made C.J. think of lazy Sunday after-
noons in the park, of eating ice cream cones under a
shade tree, of holding hands on a porch swing. She
couldn't imagine herself that comfortably relaxed, but
she could picture him that way. She toyed with the pie
on her plate and decided she might be able to finish it,
after all.

"With that huge bag of camera equipment you
carry around, I assume you're a professional photographer. You might want to get some nature shots while
you're here," he suggested, starting on his pie.

Her wariness returned. It would be safer to lie to
him again, but she looked into his eyes and found she
couldn't. What was it about his gaze that made her
want to bare her soul to him? Why was it so hard to
fight the spell of those green eyes?

"I do mostly ads and portraits," she said slowly,
"and some newspaper work. That pays the bills.
When I shoot for myself, I like the city atmosphere—
the buildings, especially the people."

"Sounds like fascinating work."

"Very. Once in Miami I came across this old Cu-
ban man sitting on a park bench feeding pigeons." She
grinned, remembering. "There was a lot of hard living in the lines of his face, but there was contentment, too. He looked like a man who'd battled a
thousand hardships and loved every minute of it."

"Those must be some photographs," Chris commented, studying her animated expression as she spoke of her work. Her eyes sparkled to life, and this time her grin was genuine and unreserved. She had a small dimple in her left cheek that would probably deepen with mischief and merriment, if she ever let go of her restraint. He wondered what it would take to get her to truly relax, and decided he wanted to be there when she did.

"The photos were magnificent. My best," she added, "but that's due mainly to the subject. Unfortunately I only got four shots before he realized I was shooting him. If I hadn't outrun the man, I wouldn't have made it home with that much."

"Outrun?"

"He chased after me, waving a broom and trying to knock the camera out of my hands. Old as he was, he managed to keep up with me for nearly ten blocks."

Chris's fork stopped halfway to his mouth. "I had no idea photography was so dangerous."

"It is when the man whose photo you take is an illegal alien." She grinned sheepishly. "At least, that's the most likely reason I can come up with for his chasing me for so long."

He laughed, then thought of her wariness around him. "I wouldn't have pegged you as such a daredevil."

"Just when photography is involved. Pictures are my passion. My apartment in D.C. is full of photographs."

Chris frowned. *D.C.?* The plates on her car were New York tags. "Business must be pretty good if you can afford a place in D.C. and another in New York."

At first his reference to New York confused her, then C.J. remembered the stolen plates on the Toyota. Her heart stopped beating, then resumed a frantic rhythm as she realized her slip of the tongue. How could she have been so careless, relaxed her guard so completely? Being alert and intelligent, of course he would spot the inconsistency when she mentioned her Washington apartment. Being a cop, he would be suspicious.

"It's Annie's car. She just moved to D.C. from New York," C.J. lied, hastily standing up. "Which reminds me, I promised her a bowl of soup and some tea. Nice to see you again, Sheriff."

Chris watched her walk to the counter, her body tense, her shoulders squared as if she were ready to fight. Or flee. At his mention of the New York license plates, her eyes had widened with fear, then she'd taken off in panic. One moment she'd been relaxed and laughing with him, the next she'd run away. But she couldn't get farther than the edge of town without transportation.

She and her sister weren't going anywhere for the moment. That gave him enough time to decide whether he should run her license plate number through the computer, just to see what turned up. He hated to go behind her back, but C.J. was obviously in some kind of trouble. Just as obviously, she wasn't about to confide in him. Not yet, anyway. Maybe it was time he knew a little more about her, he thought, studying her over the rim of his coffee cup.

Standing at the counter, C.J. felt Riker's gaze on her all the while she waited for Tammy to fill take-out containers with soup and iced tea. She knew his eyes never left her as she paid for the food and walked out.

She only hoped she hadn't made the biggest mistake of her life, letting herself relax enough to forget, even for a moment, that he was a cop.

Annie was still asleep when C.J. got back to the room. She closed the door and leaned against it, waiting for her heart rate to return to normal.

Her inbred wariness and caution had melted away under the warmth in Chris Riker's engaging smile. The man had done something few people had accomplished, and in a frighteningly short time. He'd put C.J. at ease, made her forget her reservations, her fears and uncertainties.

How had that happened?

She woke Annie and coaxed her to eat, all the while pondering why he'd gotten past her defenses. She'd had so little sleep the past two weeks. Exhaustion had made her careless. She would have to be more careful in the future.

Maybe she wouldn't see him again. At the garage, he'd called her a diversion. Maybe by morning he will have found other things to occupy his time. She clung to the hope even while she sensed its futility, even though the thought of not seeing him again made her feel oddly bereft.

Meanwhile she had Annie to think about. Her fever had continued to rise alarmingly. Her cold had settled in her chest. Her cough had become more persistent. Aspirin didn't help. She couldn't breathe, couldn't sleep. C.J. tried steaming up the bathroom to break up the congestion, but the heat was too much for Annie's fevered body. She plied her patient with liquids until Annie complained she was drowning. Still the fever didn't go down. Even cool compresses didn't help.

At three in the morning, C.J. accepted the inevitable and went downstairs, woke Shari and asked to use the phone in the hotel office. Chris Riker had insisted she call him if Annie got worse, but C.J. was reluctant to talk to him again, and she preferred not to enlist his help another time. She dialed his office number printed on the front of the card, hoping someone else would be there to take calls.

Her luck was in. A man answered, identifying himself as Deputy Oliver. He said it would take a while, but he would reach Dr. Harding and have him get in touch with her. She hung up, wondering what people in these parts did in case of emergency. Mostly, she decided, they would fend for themselves, like she generally did.

Shari sat in the office with her, though C.J. insisted it wasn't necessary. C.J. gave the appropriate responses as the other woman explained how her late husband had built the small inn, hoping the interstate would come closer to Redman than it had, but her thoughts were on Annie.

Why did she have to get sick now? Didn't she realize C.J. had all she could handle without this added complication? Annie's timing was lousy. With a stab of guilt, C.J. halted that line of thinking. Annie wasn't to blame. Still, her illness couldn't have come at a worse time.

What if she had to be hospitalized? Twice before, she'd had a cold turn into pneumonia. C.J. could remember how she and her mother had sat beside Annie's hospital bed, holding hands long into the night....

A hospital stay now would mean an additional delay getting to Seattle. Where was Matlock? Could he put out a full alert for them, or would her evidence of his criminal connections force him to limit his sources to those involved in his illegal activities? How many other agents and cops scattered throughout the country might be on the network's payroll?

There were so many unknowns, so many factors to consider, and so little margin for error.

When the phone rang, she jumped, grabbing the receiver on the first ring. But it was Chris Riker's voice that greeted her, making her heart lurch with a confusing mixture of pleasure and panic.

"The doctor is on his way." His voice, tantalizingly thick with sleep, made C.J. imagine how he would look—his rough features softened, his hair tousled, his eyes...

She banished the image, forcing herself to concentrate on her irritation with his intrusion. His deputy could have handled things without notifying him. But she should have guessed he would insist on having a finger in everything that happened in his jurisdiction. Apparently that included her. The handsome rugged sheriff had decided she would have his help whether or not she wanted it.

"Thank you, Sheriff. Sorry your deputy woke you."

The line went dead before Chris could ask C.J. how serious her sister's condition was. He replaced the receiver, then ran a hand over the stubble on his chin.

The lady clearly did not want his help. Over dinner he'd felt he was making progress with her. She had even relaxed enough to laugh and tell him a little about herself, until she'd mentioned her Washington apartment and he'd mentioned New York.

The instant, very real panic in her steely blue eyes had sent up warning flags. As did her calling the station instead of phoning him directly, after he'd told her to call him at home if she needed to reach the doctor.

No doubt about it, she was avoiding him. Wariness was necessary in a big city. He'd lived in enough of them, from Dallas to Los Angeles and points in between, to learn that. The basic mistrust, even of police officers, was the reason he'd bailed out of that rat race. But the degree of C.J.'s wariness puzzled him.

Maybe he should send her car's license plate number through the computer, after all, he thought, tugging on his sweats and running shoes. There was something fishy about her and her sister driving through rural Wyoming, and in a car that wasn't worth what the engine repairs would cost. They didn't seem interested in sight-seeing, and they didn't seem to have a particular reason for going to Billings. If they were looking for action or excitement, they wouldn't find it there.

He walked downstairs to the kitchen, stepped through the sliding glass door and onto the redwood deck. The air was cool, crisp with the scent of pine. The sky was barely beginning to gray. The moon had retired and the sun hadn't quite raised its sleepy head. Chris walked down the steps and rapped lightly on the door at the side of the garage. There was a sniffing sound, followed by the faint outline of a dark canine head pushing through the cutout in the door.

"Come on, Charlemagne," he said softly. "It's early, but I'm awake, so we might as well get moving."

The Doberman ambled up to be scratched behind the ears, yawned, then proceeded to stretch while Chris did his own stretching exercises. When he started down the gravel driveway at an easy trot, the dog was at his side. They traveled the roads every day, so they had no problem finding their way in the semidarkness.

C.J. was one nervous lady, Chris decided, picking up his pace. There could be a dozen reasons for it, criminal and otherwise. "Most likely otherwise," he said to the dog running at his side. "I could be wrong, but my hunch is she's honest. And if she'd done something illegal, she would be risking a lot by taking that overly talkative sister of hers on the lam."

By the time he'd finished his ritual three miles, Chris had decided that whatever C.J.'s problem was— whether she was escaping an unpleasant relationship, or taking her younger sister out of a bad situation—he wanted to hear it from her. He wanted her to trust him enough to tell him what was wrong. He doubted it would be easy to gain her confidence in the few days she would be stranded in Redman, but nowadays he took his challenges where he found them.

Meanwhile, it couldn't hurt to find out what he could about her on his own. Starting with the tags on her car.

As always before, Keith answered the phone on the first ring. C.J. sighed in relief at hearing her friend's voice again. He was her lifeline, the only person with whom she could discuss her fears.

"How could you have done that?" he asked in near panic at her mention of her blunder at dinner last night. "What if this Riker decides to make sure that

Annie used to live in New York and moved to D.C. like you said?''

''He doesn't know our surname. How much checking could he do?'' she asked, needing to know how much damage she'd done.

''He could run a make on those stolen plates.''

C.J. had thought of that. All the while she'd nursed Annie, she'd expected Chris Riker to barge through the door to arrest them. So far that hadn't happened.

''I think if he'd done that, Annie and I would be in jail by now,'' she said. ''He must have believed me.''

''Maybe, but that's no guarantee he won't suddenly decide to run a make on you.''

C.J. rubbed a hand over her sleep-deprived eyes. She'd agonized over her blunder and over Annie's health more hours than she cared to count. She was so tired of worrying. ''I know. But what can I do to minimize the damage?''

There was a long moment of silence, then Keith growled in frustration. ''Nothing, I guess. Meanwhile, I've made copies of the evidence you expressed to me a few days ago. I gave them to some people I can trust. In case anything happens . . .''

C.J. straightened in her chair. ''Why? What's going on?'' *Had Matlock made the connection between her and Keith?*

''It's just a precaution. I don't think Jennings is on to my probing into his past, but you can never be positive. I want to have some insurance, that's all.''

''Survival instinct,'' she muttered.

''Right.''

''Will these people you gave the papers to be able to do anything about our 'friends'?''

"They've got some heavy clout. They'll start a scandal that Jordainne won't be able to cover up. When he goes down, he won't go alone. The whole network will fall with him. And Matlock will be one of the first."

"Then why don't we let them handle things?" she asked with an uncustomary need to dump her problem in someone else's lap. She was afraid and so tired of trying to hide her fear, to keep it under control.

"Because that wouldn't assure your safety. We've got to get you someplace where you can have protection first."

He was right, but that meant she would be forced to handle the strain for several more days. And nights. Nights were the worst. She was afraid to close her eyes, and when she did, the nightmarish dreams were always there.

At least Annie would be all right. The doctor had given her a penicillin shot and was sending out prescriptions tomorrow, or rather later today. That was one less problem on C.J.'s mind.

"Will these people believe Jordainne is a criminal?" she asked Keith.

"They'll have doubts. Hell, that's only natural, considering his popularity. But they'll check him out. Thoroughly. And they'll expose him for the scum he is."

The conversational pause that followed had an ominous feel, C.J. thought. "If you've got bad news, let's have it."

It took a moment before Keith spoke up. "Your car. The Ford," he clarified. "I had a buddy check on it. Strictly on the quiet." He paused again.

"And?" C.J. prompted, braced for the blow.

"Matlock found it."

She mulled over the news for an instant, then brightened. "If he's just now found it, that means he's not even close—"

"He found it several days ago. The day after you ditched it."

The fear clamped its tight hand over her heart again. "Did he get any leads on me?"

"All my friend could tell me is that they did a thorough search of the area. He didn't know what they came up with." Keith waited. When she made no response, he continued, "Most likely Matlock got nothing. You took all the precautions I told you to take, right?"

"Yeah." While C.J. followed in her own vehicle, Annie had driven the newly purchased Toyota two hundred miles west. They'd left C.J.'s Ford in one of the parking stalls of a sprawling mall.

"Then let's not worry about it. If Matlock hasn't shown up by now..."

That didn't mean he wasn't slowly, methodically closing in on her, C.J. knew, and she and Annie had no means of getting away. Why had she ever thought having the car repaired would be the safer of the two evils?

She breathed deeply to steady her inner trembling. "How's your check into Jennings coming?"

"Still nothing conclusive. The man's a name-dropper, but there's nothing criminal about wanting to impress people. He lives in style, but supposedly his wife inherited quite a bit of money."

"And inheriting's not illegal. Keith, how much longer?"

"I'll step up things as much as I can." When she sighed, he said, "I know it's tough for you. Just hang in there a little longer."

As she replaced the receiver, she muttered, "Hang in there. The story of my life."

Chapter 3

Annie sat up in bed and pointed to the hotel door. "Out, C.J. I mean it."

"Annie, be reasonable. I don't like leaving you alone."

"*You* be reasonable. Nothing's going to happen to me, except between this cough and your endless pacing keeping me awake, I'm going to go crazy." She flopped back on the pillows. "When is the drugstore in that other town supposed to deliver the prescriptions the doctor ordered?"

"Soon." C.J. stared out the window at the tall, unbending fir trees and the cloudless blue sky. The breeze would be cool, but the afternoon sun would be warm and bright. Most photographers preferred overcast days when shadows were at a minimum, but C.J. enjoyed the challenge of working with the contrasts.

Redman's weathered buildings against the patches of dark would make some interesting pictures. How long had it been since she'd had the luxury to indulge in her curiosity and creativity? Only a week, but it felt like a year. Annie's cough brought C.J.'s thoughts back to the problems facing them. She paced to the bed and back.

Annie groaned. "You're doing it again." Before C.J. realized her intent, Annie jumped out of bed, grabbed the camera bag by the shoulder strap and pulled and shoved the heavy case out into the hallway.

"What are you doing?"

C.J. rushed forward to retrieve the bag, but Annie stood in the doorway, facing her older sister. "I'm throwing you out. Between this cough, the fever and the running, I haven't had a decent night's sleep in a week. You've been pushing me to the limit, and I've had it."

"This hasn't exactly been a picnic for me, either."

"I know." Coughing, Annie walked over to the bed and sank down wearily. "And I haven't forgotten it's my fault we're in this mess in the first place. If I hadn't appointed myself a one-woman crusader to expose that worm Jordainne, we wouldn't be here now."

"I understand why you felt you had to do it. You're very honest and sort of naive and impulsive," C.J. said sympathetically. Her sister had inherited those traits from their father. Nothing had changed those aspects of his personality and C.J. doubted Annie would ever change, either.

"Which is a nice way of saying I don't always stop to think things through before I act." Annie brushed the hair back from her forehead. "You warned me about Jordainne's connections, but an FBI agent . . ."

"Matlock's not the first cop on the take."

"I know you're right. Thank heaven you made copies of the evidence I turned over to him. Otherwise we'd never get anyone to believe us."

"With the senator's carefully manufactured reputation, it won't be easy to make people believe he's working for criminals, even with the evidence."

"You warned me of that, too. I swear, the next time you tell me I'm doing something rash, I'll listen."

C.J. smiled to herself. Annie had said those same words many times before, though none of the other incidents had had life-threatening consequences. When Annie coughed again, C.J. stepped into the hallway and bent down to pick up the camera bag.

Straightening, she looked up into Chris Riker's green eyes. He stood at the top of the stairs, one foot on the landing.

Her stomach knotted as she mentally replayed her conversation with Annie. Had he overheard them?

"Sheriff," she said cautiously.

He met her suspicion with one of his warm smiles. "Afternoon, ma'am. Brought by the medicine Doc ordered for your little sister." He tipped his hat, the gesture and his drawl an irresistible imitation of a lawman straight out of an Old West movie, and held out a white paper sack.

C.J. set the camera bag inside the room and leaned against the doorjamb.

Like the heroine saved from the villain's clutches, she wanted to throw herself at his feet. His fitted uniform hugged his broad firm chest and muscled thighs in a way that left very little to her imagination. He radiated an aura of raw masculinity and power. In a matter of seconds she knew which lenses and light settings she would use to shoot him in that pose. But this wasn't a studio shoot and he wasn't a male model in a sheriff's uniform. He was the real thing.

Reluctantly she pulled her straying thoughts back in line. "Doctor Harding said the drugstore in North-field would deliver it."

Chris stifled his frustration with her. Getting to know C.J. was not going to be easy, but he was nothing if not determined. "My office is across the street from the pharmacy."

"Yes," she prompted, eyeing him intently.

"I stopped in to buy a candy bar and Mr. Parker mentioned he didn't have any other deliveries coming this way. So I volunteered."

"At this rate, I'll never be able to pay off on all the rewards I owe you."

"That's kinda what I had in mind." Chris wasn't above using her obvious need to repay her debts to his advantage. It would be his one and only hook to get her to spend some time with him. She was the most interesting female he'd come across in a long time. He wasn't letting her go until he explored this attraction. He inclined his head toward the room. "How is she?"

"Still feverish and coughing. The doctor said it's a bad case of bronchitis. He gave her a shot, and with this medicine she'll be better in a day or two."

"If I ever *get* any of that medicine," Annie called out from the bed.

With a sigh, C.J. took the sack, carried it to the nightstand, gave Annie one of the antibiotic capsules, then the cough syrup. She sank back onto the bed and pulled the blankets up to her chin. C.J. glanced at the receipt, took some cash from her purse and walked back to the door.

"Thank you. Again." She handed Chris the money.

"No problem." Chris pocketed the bills, studying her stiff posture and wondering what the check on her license plates would turn up. As he'd expected, a local check had turned up nothing, so he would have to wait for a nationwide computer check. Small town offices were on the bottom of that priority list, but with any luck he would have an answer in a day or two. Meanwhile, he hoped he could get her to talk about whatever it was that had her running scared.

"Why did you call my office when you needed Doc?" he asked. "I said you could call me at home."

"I didn't want to disturb you when your deputy could do the job." There'd been more to it than that. All the while she'd nursed Annie, C.J. had remembered how relaxed she'd felt with him at dinner. That and the memory of her slip of the tongue scared her. She couldn't take the risk of spending time with him. But his charm, and her own attraction to it, made maintaining any distance difficult.

"Around here we don't consider our neighbors are disturbing us when they ask for help." His smile softened the serious tone in his voice. "Besides, as your rescuer, it's my privilege to look after you."

His choice of phrase made C.J. bristle. "Thank you, Sheriff, but I can—"

"Manage. You've pointed that out several times."

"And you seem determined to ignore it. Does a capable female intimidate you?"

"Now who is psychoanalyzing without a license?"

"C...J." Annie ground out the name.

"Problems?" Chris cast a concerned glance at the door.

"Yes," Annie called out before C.J. could answer. "I need sleep. Sheriff—"

"Call me Chris."

"Chris, then. Take C.J. somewhere and don't be in any hurry to bring her back."

"Annie!"

"I could arrest her for disturbing the peace," he offered, chuckling at the way things were playing into his hand. He wanted time with C.J., and her sister was determined to give it to him.

"No, nothing so drastic. Take her somewhere, anywhere. Just promise you'll keep her out of here for the afternoon."

"Sure thing." He grinned down at C.J., noting the alarm and awareness in her eyes. "I need to see Johnny Brave Hawk at the feed store. You can come along. Johnny's a sucker for a pretty lady with a camera."

The Indian name captured C.J.'s attention, though she didn't miss the compliment Chris had thrown in. She shouldn't spend more time with him, but the chance to photograph someone named Johnny Brave Hawk made her shutter finger itch. Surely Annie would be safe. In the five-block town, C.J. wouldn't be far away, and she would only be gone an hour or so. During that time, though, she would be on her guard constantly. She couldn't risk another slipup like last night's.

"Let me get my camera." She shouldered the bag, said a quick goodbye to her cranky patient and closed the door behind her.

"That equipment must weigh a ton," Chris said, leading the way down the stairs. He wanted to give her a hand with the heavy bag, but knew better than to ask. "Haven't you ever heard of pocket cameras?"

C.J.'s expression was pained. "Someone should teach you the difference between photographs and amateur snapshots."

"Like a professional photographer, maybe?"

"Okay," she said, recognizing the challenge. "With a really good photograph, it's like actually being there. You see sun reflected off a building and *feel* sweaty and hot. You see a face and feel the pain or contentment etched in the lines. A snapshot is only a hazy memory." She shrugged. "I'd give you a visual demonstration, but I left my portfolio at home."

"Maybe you'll decide to come back this way. Sometime when you can stay awhile." He opened the door for her, holding his breath. Though he didn't understand why her answer should be so important, it was. He wanted to know the need to explore this attraction between them was mutual. But her only answer was a small noncommittal smile.

C.J. stepped past him and onto the sunlit sidewalk, wondering why the idea of returning appealed to her. Since leaving Mason Falls after her father's death, she'd gone out of her way to avoid small towns. But Redman seemed different. It was smaller than Mason Falls. Rougher, too. No attractive, misleading surface veneer, just stark honesty. The weather-beaten buildings gave silent testimony to the harshness of life here, but to strength and endurance, also. The paint might be cracked and peeling, but the foundations were solid.

The man at her side belonged here. He was rugged enough to withstand anything life in this area threw at him. And he would do it with his warmth and his invincible humor.

As they crossed the street and approached the store, she decided she'd better change the subject, and the direction of her thoughts. "Does your friend work here?"

"He and his two sons own the store." Chris opened the door and called to the man behind the counter.

Johnny Brave Hawk was all C.J. had hoped for. With his prominent features, his lifelined face, alert dark eyes and straight, graying raven hair, he could have posed for any of the aged photos her father had collected, painstakingly restored and preserved. As soon as they were introduced, C.J. set the bag at her feet and pulled out the Nikon. Chris leaned against the counter, watching while she took readings with a light meter, then adjusted the settings on the Nikon.

"At one time my ancestors believed the camera would steal their souls." Johnny chuckled. "Of course, they also believed the white man's promises."

C.J. nodded. "It's difficult to know whom to trust."

Trust. She'd taken Johnny's words seriously, Chris thought, watching her work. Trust didn't come easy for her. Before settling in Wyoming, the same had been true for him. Growing up in a series of foster homes in the toughest parts of Dallas, he'd learned that few people kept their word.

But from what little she'd told him about her father, Chris gathered C.J.'s background wasn't as rough and loveless as his own. So where had she come by her instinctive mistrust? One more piece of the intriguing puzzle that she was. Chris filed the thought away as he and Johnny talked about the break-in at the store last night.

"Do you have many break-ins?" she asked from behind the camera lens.

Chris thought he detected an unusual amount of tension in her voice, and wondered at it. "Just occasional problems like this. From the amateurish look of things, I'd guess it was kids who didn't have anything better to do."

He thought he noticed her shoulders relax somewhat as she started on a second roll of film. Chris was fascinated with her graceful and quick movements, with how she always seemed to know just what she was looking for. Her current subject was Johnny's four-year-old grandson. She got down on her knees and elbows and angled the camera up at him, giving Chris another enticing view of her sexy bottom. Joey, the block tower he was building, even the conversation with Johnny, was forgotten, with her in that provocative pose. He felt his chest constrict.

Then the tower tumbled. C.J. got four shots in rapid-fire succession, each from a different angle, capturing the boy's surprise, then his alarm and dismay, and finally his laughter, all before the last block hit the floor. Then with a speed that caught Chris off guard, she spun around and got three of him.

"You're a little slow on the draw, Sheriff," she said in a lazy drawl. She came to a sitting position, laughing as she folded her legs under her.

Chris saw the mischievous gleam in her eyes and vowed he would see it again. It was all he'd anticipated it would be. The dimple in her cheek deepened captivatingly.

"Yeah, well, around here when we have a shootout, we do it at high noon on Main Street, not in the feed store's office." He grinned.

Still laughing, C.J. repacked her equipment and said goodbye to Johnny and Joey, who was devouring the candy bar Chris had passed him. Out on the street, Chris walked close to her, his hand on her arm.

Protective. He didn't understand it, but that was definitely how he felt toward her. The way she'd come so alert at his mention of the break-in, the way she'd relaxed when he said it was an amateur operation, the way she was so guarded around him, he had a strong hunch she was running from someone. He wanted to be the one she ran to for help. Sometime soon he would have to analyze the crazy emotions she made him feel and decide what he was going to do about them. She wouldn't be in Redman for long.

C.J. felt the warmth of his hand on her arm and wondered why she didn't subtly, but firmly, distance herself from him. With anyone else the proprietary gesture would annoy her, but with Chris there was a bewildering enjoyment of his attentiveness. As involved as she'd been with photographing her subjects in the store, she'd been very aware of his eyes on her. More than once she'd caught his lingering gaze, recognized the barely concealed desire in the dark green depths. The look had been unmistakable when she'd caught him by surprise and turned the camera on him.

What concerned her now was the way her feminine instincts responded to that combination of awareness, fascination and appreciation in his eyes. It beckoned to her, made her feel warm, alive, intrigued. A complication she didn't need just now.

But the more she was with Chris Riker, the more interested she became. He wasn't just another ruggedly good-looking man with an engaging sense of humor and an irresistible smile, she thought, walking down the street with him. He had substance, character. From the conversation in the feed store it was clear Johnny respected Chris and valued his opinions.

That morning Shari had spoken at length on the sheriff's virtues. The people of the dozen small towns in his jurisdiction relied on him for more than law enforcement. Though C.J. had been worried about Annie, she'd stayed to hear Shari's recitation of his accomplishments since winning his first election, seven years ago. C.J. had left the office wondering if the young widow wasn't in love with the handsome sheriff. She'd wondered herself how it would be to know him under different circumstances, and had decided she would enjoy it.

"You're awfully quiet," Chris said as they turned down a little street that ran behind the grocery store.

C.J. blushed, realizing she'd been completely engaged with the prospects playing in her mind, but figured his ego didn't need boosting. "Just wondering if Annie is awake."

"We have a couple more stops to make, then we'll head back and check on her."

He'd assumed complete command over her afternoon, C.J. thought with a frown. As much as she enjoyed his company, she couldn't afford to forget the need for caution. She was becoming too relaxed with him, far too comfortable. Very dangerous. Another slip of the tongue like last night's could spell certain disaster for her and for Annie.

"Sheriff, why don't I leave you to your work and go off on my own? I can hardly get lost."

"I promised your sister I'd keep you busy."

"Yes, but you didn't come to Redman just to spend the afternoon with me."

"I did hope to get you to tag along. But regardless, I won't break a promise. Tell you what," he continued, the hesitation he sensed in her strengthening his resolve not to let her back out of their afternoon together. "We'll flip a coin. Heads you come with me, tails I go with you."

C.J.'s laughter escaped before she could catch it. Looking up into his grin, she felt the fight go out of her. She didn't want to be alone—a startling discovery for someone who'd been a loner most of her life. No matter how risky it might be, she wanted to spend time with him, to experience more of his quiet wit, and cocky smiles. Besides, he'd made it clear he would persevere until he got what he wanted. She would have to be extra cautious.

"Forget the coin, Sheriff. I'll come peaceably."

"Want some help with that bag?"

She shook her head. As long as Jordainne's ledger and diary sheets were stashed under the camera equipment, no one else would get near it.

"Sure?" he pressed.

C.J. raised her eyes heavenward. "And I used to think persistence was a virtue."

His warm laughter washed over her, captivating and awakening her senses. As they finished making his rounds that afternoon, she found herself craving the sound of it, reveling in it, and in his deep, velvet voice. She could listen to him for hours, the way she'd listened to her dad tell stories about the Old West. Chris had that same kind of voice, entrancing, easy on the ears.

If only she could stifle some of his questions, she thought as they left the little residential area tucked behind the grocery store. She was suddenly tired of having to weigh every word before saying it.

"I overheard you tell Mattie Foster's daughter you've moved around a lot since your dad's death," Chris said as they headed back to the hotel. "Part of your work?"

"More a case of restlessness. Always searching for more than a small town has to offer." She had yet to find the place she wanted to be on a permanent basis, and had come to think maybe it didn't exist for her. Noting the early-evening air had cooled, C.J. pulled her jean jacket around her. "Have you lived here all your life?"

"I grew up in Dallas," Chris said after a long moment's debate whether to pursue his line of questioning. He wanted to know more about her, but she was the most evasive person he'd ever met. He didn't want to push so hard he lost her. "Once I was on my own, though, I did my share of moving around."

Relieved he hadn't turned the conversation back to her, C.J. let out the breath she'd been holding. "After living where it's warm and sunny, why did you pick someplace that's frigid nine months out of the year?"

He laughed. "Sugar, first there was Dallas, then I toured even hotter spots courtesy of Uncle Sam, then came home to do a few years in the desert southwest. I took my police training in Albuquerque, and after a while I moved to Santa Fe, then from there to L.A. and then to Phoenix with a few stops in between. When Phoenix lost its glamour, I moved on to San Diego in the summer."

"I'm beginning to get the picture."

"Mmm. You want hot, there's no place like the city streets in the summer. Tempers are short, tension is high and you never stop sweating. I did that scene for too many years.''

''Why didn't you bail out sooner?''

''I was trying to prove to myself that I had staying power somewhere. But each day the work got more frustrating. There were always more criminals than we could put away, and the system had our hands tied much of the time. Then one really hot day that last year, I nearly lost it.'' He sighed deeply, as if the memories weighed heavily on him.

''What happened?''

''My partner and I were trying to cuff some kid and he pulled a switchblade. Sliced down the side of my arm. I managed to keep my cool while we subdued him and during the ride to the station, but it took every bit of self-control I possessed and then some to keep from taking out years worth of frustration on him.''

C.J. gasped. The at-his-limit man he spoke of then was so at odds with the serene man walking beside her.

''That incident made me do some serious thinking,'' he continued. ''I'd been in police work for eight years, in nearly as many cities, and I hadn't made a damned bit of difference anywhere. There was no one in my life I really cared about, and no one who cared a hell of a lot what happened to me. Things weren't working out and it was time for a change, as my marine drill instructor used to say.''

''You were in the Marines?''

He smiled wryly. ''I was a real delinquent as a kid until I got into some trouble I couldn't talk my way out of and the judge gave me a choice between jail or the service. I signed up the next day.''

The rough reputation of the Marines would have appealed to him, she thought, casting a glance at his rugged profile. "Bet that was an education."

"It was. How about you? Where'd you grow up?"

"Mason Falls, Nebraska. Population around a thousand."

"About the size of Northfield."

C.J. inhaled the unpolluted air, cool and fragrant, and realized she'd forgotten how good smog-free air could smell. The setting sun cast a pink glow on the few gray clouds that lined the horizon. "This part of Wyoming is beautiful, and the people... I like them."

"Around here you're judged by who you are, what you do, not lumped in some category."

"Like cop?"

"Yeah. Nobody trusts a cop these days."

C.J.'s eyebrow rose at the hint of bitterness in his tone. "You shouldn't take it personally."

"I know. No matter what the profession, there are people you can trust and others you can't." And she didn't trust anyone, he thought. She was still dodging his attempts to learn more about her. Getting her to open up was going to take more time than he'd anticipated, and time was something he didn't have an excess of. "Here," he went on to say, "I've really gotten to know the people."

"And here you're in charge." That would be important to him, too, C.J. thought as they approached the hotel.

"You picked up on that, did you?" Grinning, he pushed open the door and held it for her.

"I enjoyed the afternoon, Sheriff." So much that she was reluctant to say goodbye, though she should be glad to part company with him. She paused, one foot on the bottom step, feeling as if she stood on the edge of a cliff.

"Your sister didn't have any trouble calling me Chris."

"Annie never does," she hedged, feeling pulled closer to the brink, feeling dizzy with the emotions warring inside her.

"And you don't?"

"Not until I've known someone awhile."

"Have dinner with me and I'll try to convince you to make an exception in my case." From the diner's kitchen came the aroma of Shari's cooking. He inhaled deeply. "Pot roast tonight."

C.J. smiled at his contagious enthusiasm, and felt herself fall the rest of the way. "Where else could I go without transportation? And if I refuse, you'll join me, anyway. That doesn't leave me much choice."

"You could always try room service, if you wanted to avoid my company."

But she didn't. She'd hoped he would ask. Giving in to her rare daring streak wasn't wise just now, but she couldn't help herself. "Let me check on Annie, though."

"Have her join us if she feels up to it."

"I'll ask."

Annie didn't stir when C.J. entered the room, or when she stashed the camera bag under the bed. She was still sleeping when C.J. left the room ten minutes later. When she walked into the diner, Chris was at the counter talking to Shari, smiling fondly into her dark brown eyes.

Seeing Shari return that look, C.J. hesitated at the doorway. She didn't want to intrude on the scene, but she didn't want to see Chris gaze at the other woman with such open friendliness, either. She wanted to run away, wanted to barge in and demand his attention. Before she could make sense of her conflicting emotions, he turned and spotted her. His smile perceptibly warmer, he led her to a booth by the window.

As she slid into the seat, Chris got another whiff of her perfume—a subtle floral scent, light, delicate and captivating. It had tantalized his senses all afternoon, sending his thoughts skittering wildly.

He sat down across from her. "Is Annie coming?"

C.J. shook her head. "She was asleep and I wasn't brave enough to wake her."

"A wise decision considering how adamant she was about not being disturbed."

Shari took their orders, returning several minutes later with two pot roast dinners, tea and coffee. Chris went through the motions of talking and eating, but C.J. was a constant distraction.

She was slender—small breasts, tiny waist and narrow hips—but there was nothing fragile about her. He sensed she had an inner strength and determination that might rival his own. That only added to his growing interest in her.

The red highlights in her chestnut hair shimmered. She'd brushed the strands back and fastened them behind one ear with an antique-gold clip. The style was inviting. Chris longed to tug the old-fashioned clip out, to sample her soft curls as they cascaded over his hand. He reached for his coffee cup, surprised and intrigued by the direction of his thoughts. When had interest turned to such burning desire?

Knowing when wasn't important, he decided when she laughed at something he'd said. It had happened and more than ever he wanted a chance to explore it.

He was glad Annie had been asleep. He wanted C.J. to himself for as long as possible.

Long after they'd finished their meal and the other customers in the diner had left, he and C.J. sat talking. He noted with very definite satisfaction that the wariness in her eyes was finally gone. As she finished her tea, he recounted the story of his first adventure camping in Yellowstone. When he described the two days of solid rain, the leaky backpack and leakier tent, soggy food, wet ground and wetter clothes, she laughed. He found himself embellishing the story so he could hear the sound again and again.

"The closest I've come to camping out was a rest stop in South Carolina," she said, traces of laughter lingering in her voice. "I slept in my car because I was dead tired and down to my last twenty dollars, with no job prospects."

"Do you travel that way often?" Chris was surprised at the protective streak that surged through him again. He didn't like her casual shrug.

"That was the brief period in my life when I was on my own. Dad was gone, Annie was situated at college and I was just going professional with my photography. I spent every spare penny of my meager income on equipment. I still spend a lot on it, but my finances have improved slightly. Now I generally have about thirty dollars on me, sometimes thirty-five."

Chris started to comment on safety precautions for a woman traveling alone, then caught the gleam in her eyes and stopped. "You're baiting me, aren't you?"

She grinned. "I could see the lecture coming."

"That's entrapment." Laughing, he grabbed her hand and led her up to the cash register.

With her thoughts caught up with the warmth of his touch, the strength of his grip, C.J. barely noticed him taking out enough money to cover their meal and the tip.

"Chris, on top of everything else you've done for me, I can't let you buy dinner," she protested when he laid the bills on the counter.

"You don't have a choice. I'm bigger than you are—"

She leaned one elbow on the counter and eyed him up and down, from the rugged features of his handsome face, to the breadth of his shoulders and torso, to his firm hips—admiring all she saw. "Yes, but—"

"I'm also the law in these parts."

"Can't argue with that."

"And this way, you still owe me. Hopefully once you finish your business in Billings, whatever it is, you'll feel obliged to return and repay the debt."

He'd read her perfectly on that point, C.J. admitted to herself as they walked through the doorway and into the hotel lobby. She didn't like to owe anyone because it gave that person a hold over you. Like now, with Chris. She sensed his mention of Billings was a subtle attempt to pry information from her—why she was going there of all places, how long she'd be there and where she would head after that. His pushing, though, would gain him nothing but another evasive reply.

She arched one brow. "That's blackmail."

"Yeah, but who's going to arrest the sheriff?"

He flashed that grin C.J. was getting to know quite well. During dinner she'd found herself studying his smile as if she were about to photograph it, turning her head slightly to look at it from all possible angles, mentally deciding which poses would show the various aspects of his personality to the fullest. The way the one corner of his mouth lifted and the lines there and around his eyes deepened was entrancing. Each angle seemed to show another facet of that smile—amusement, self-assurance, vitality, virility. She could shoot it a dozen times and catch something new in each frame.

At the foot of the stairs, she turned to thank him again, but the look in his eyes stopped her before she could start. The longing she'd glimpsed at the feed store was there again, very plain and equally undeniable. She felt a tingle travel up her arm as he took her hand in his. Standing on the bottom step, her eyes almost level with his, she knew he meant to kiss her.

"Chris, I don't think this is a good idea."

"But it's what I've wanted to do all afternoon."

His gentle smile told her he understood her hesitation and uncertainty. His quiet words told her he wouldn't back down unless she insisted. But she didn't have the power.

He leaned closer, his breath fanning her cheek. She couldn't let him kiss her. She couldn't let him go until he had. Logic gave way to longing. Caution gave way to curiosity.

His mouth was so close, yet it seemed to take forever to reach hers. In that instant she realized how much she wanted his kiss. Then his lips touched hers and there was room only for thoughts of him. She inhaled the pine-needle scent of his cologne. She felt the warmth from his body reach out to her, felt the gentle tug of his hand in her hair, the firm pressure of his fingertips on her back as he held her against him.

His muscled chest was hard and unyielding. His lips were tender and giving. The hint of his beard was tantalizingly rough against her soft skin. The brush of his tongue against her lower lip lit a flame deep within her. Heat rushed through her veins. C.J. experienced each sensation distinctly and individually before they blended and blurred, drawing her deeper into the haze that had wrapped around her.

Chris went slowly, not wanting to frighten her with the strength of his need. He'd wanted before, but never with such immediacy, such intensity. To hold back hurt, but to give in totally to the desire pulsating through his veins was to risk losing what little he had of her.

She was unbelievably warm and responsive, more than he'd ever imagined. At another touch of his tongue her mouth opened. She moaned softly as he deepened the kiss. Her breasts pressed against his chest, her curves molded to him, her arms wound around his neck, holding him tightly.

He breathed in her scent—delicate, unique. He lost his fingers in the soft tumble of curls he held. He luxuriated in the heat radiating from her slender body. Then, dimly aware he was reaching the limit of his own endurance, he pulled his mouth from hers.

"You were wrong, C.J. This was a very good idea, very good." Not yet ready to break the contact completely, he nuzzled her ear. The scent of her perfume was stronger there. He doubted anything would ever satisfy his sense of smell so completely. "We'll spend the day together tomorrow. I'll take you horseback riding."

"Mmm." His lips were warm, gentle, caressing. C.J. sighed, too preoccupied with the kisses he trailed down her neck to be concerned with what he said. So preoccupied, she was surprised when she heard another voice and felt him release her.

"Oh, Chris, I didn't know you were still here." He straightened and turned toward Shari, who stood in the doorway. "Oh, I . . . I'm sorry," she said, glimpsing C.J. "I didn't mean to intrude."

"You're not," Chris told her. "I was just leaving." He gave C.J. a quick smile. "Tomorrow. Bye, Shari."

"See ya," she said, watching the door close. With a sigh, she tossed her long black hair over one shoulder. "As Grandma used to say, a gal could do a lot worse."

"I, uh . . ." C.J. searched for words to explain the situation. She hadn't meant for the kiss to happen, but she hadn't had the will to stop it. The thought that there could be something between him and Shari had vanished from C.J.'s mind the minute he'd pulled her into his arms. But her presence in Redman was only temporary. She didn't have any right to encourage Chris's attentions, to get in Shari's way.

"It's all right," Shari said as if she sensed C.J.'s uneasiness. "Chris and I tried it once, but I can't seem to forget about Jack."

"Your late husband?" C.J. asked softly.

Shari nodded, wiping her hands on her apron. "I came to ask if your sister wanted anything to eat before I closed up for the night. She's had so little today, I thought she might like a slice of roast and some mashed potatoes."

"Thanks. I'm sure she'll be hungry." Reluctantly C.J. pulled her thoughts back to the other problems she still had to deal with, ones that had come along before Chris Riker, ones that would still be there long after she'd left Redman, and him. "May I make another long-distance call while you fix the plate? I'll find out the charges and reimburse you again."

"Sure. Use the phone anytime you want. I'll leave the plate on the counter."

As Shari walked back to the diner, C.J. turned toward the office. Sitting behind the desk, she reached for the black phone and dialed the prearranged number. After three tries there was still no answer. Keith had told her this might happen, and if it did, to wait an hour and try again.

His not being there the first time shouldn't worry her, but C.J.'s stomach knotted just the same. If he were there, he would say that anxiety was counterproductive. If only she could turn it off, she thought as she walked out of the office and headed for the diner.

Shari had retired for the night, but she'd left the covered dish and a glass of tea on the spotlessly clean counter. Getting Annie well enough to travel was the only problem C.J. could do anything about at the moment, so she would concentrate on that instead of Keith's absence. It was the only way she would hang on to her sanity. She carried the plate upstairs, balancing it and the glass as she opened the room door. The nightstand lamp was on.

"About time you got back." Spotting the food, Annie threw back the blankets, scrambled to a sitting position and reached for the plate. She greedily pulled off the aluminum-foil cover and inhaled. "Oh, heaven. You read my mind."

C.J. watched Annie dig into the potatoes and gravy. "You must be feeling better."

"Some. My chest still aches a little," she mumbled between mouthfuls. "You been with Chris all this time?"

"Yeah." C.J. sat on the other bed. Chris Riker was another problem she wasn't sure how to handle. She couldn't leave town, as she usually did when a man got uncomfortably close. Not until the car was repaired, at least. Meanwhile, she had no doubt she would be seeing more of the sheriff.

"What'd you do besides see the guy at the feed store?"

"We had dinner downstairs."

Annie cast a quick glance at C.J. "Really? What'd you do in between that and the feed store?"

C.J. sighed, realizing Annie wasn't going to give up easily. "I went with him while he talked to Mattie Foster about tying up her dog so it doesn't chase rabbits through Mr. Thompson's vegetable garden. Her daughter wouldn't let me leave until I gave her an interview." C.J. chuckled as Annie's eyes widened in surprise. "I'm going to be the subject of an eighth grade English composition."

"Wow. When you're famous, will you still remember me?" Annie's eyes sparkled.

"Shut up and take your medicine." Laughing, C.J. pitched the prescription bottle toward the other bed. With a soft plop, it landed beside Annie's leg.

"So what do you think of Chris?" Annie popped one of the pills in her mouth and set the bottle on the nightstand.

C.J. shrugged. "He's nice."

Annie gave a short, disgusted sigh. "I fix you up with a gorgeous guy and all you can say is, 'He's nice.'"

"Fix me up?" C.J. repeated indignantly. "You threw me at him."

"And for that you'll be forever in my debt."

In a flash C.J. was on her feet. Hands planted on her hips, and eyes narrowed, she stared into Annie's laughing expression. "He's a cop. Do you know the trouble he could cause us? You're lucky I don't smother you with a pillow."

"You and who else? You really like him, don't you?"

With only a growl for an answer, C.J. headed for the bathroom and a hot shower. Sisters knew each other too well, she thought, pulling off her clothes. At least, she and Annie had never been able to keep secrets from each other for long.

But the kiss on the stairs was one secret C.J. planned to keep, at least until she knew what to make of her reaction to it. She'd never been so carried away in a man's arms before. That it had happened now, with him, and so completely... That would take some thinking about.

Yes, she liked Chris, she admitted as the hot water cascaded over her shoulders. Liked him a lot. But it was the wrong time and wrong place. Until she finished the Jordainne business Annie had handed her, she couldn't take time to explore the attraction. And as for the place— How long could she be content in any town where she didn't even need a wide-angle lens to photograph the skyline, and where a new face was rarer than a January thaw in the arctic?

From the phone in the hotel office, C.J. once again tried the number Keith had given her. After twelve rings she hung up, waited five minutes, then tried again. And again. For thirty minutes she continued to call the number, but there was no answer. With each call the knot in her stomach twisted and tightened.

Where was Keith? He'd assured her if he missed the first call, he would be there to take the second one. Without fail, he'd said.

Had something gone wrong? She had the right number, she knew. Keith had given her the schedule, then they'd double-checked dates, times and numbers to make sure there were no errors. Why wasn't he there to answer the phone? She had to know, had to take a chance on tracking him down.

She dialed his office at the newspaper first, only to be told he'd been out all day. With mounting trepidation, she dialed his home number. She knew the risks she was taking. He'd lectured her often enough about wire taps. But if something had happened to him... She had to know. Her life and Annie's might depend on it.

"Hello." The voice was female. Keith's wife, C.J. assumed.

"Hi. May I speak with Mr. Taylor?"

"No, he isn't here," Mrs. Taylor snapped. "He promised to be home for dinner. But as usual..."

Tensing at the woman's concern behind the angry words, C.J. asked, "Is he working late?"

"I don't know. He doesn't answer his pager."

She winced as her stomach muscles twisted until they couldn't knot any more.

"Do you want to leave a message?" the other woman asked.

C.J. debated. She couldn't leave her name, but she had to let Keith know she'd tried to reach him, had to do something to make sure he would be there to an-

swer her next call. Then she remembered the code
name they had invented.

"Tell him Mr. Wexler's secretary called," she said,
"and that I'll call again in the morning."

She hung up the phone and sat back in the squeaky
wooden chair, chewing her lower lip. Keith's absence
could mean a dozen things, she reminded herself,
nearly all of them perfectly natural in a city the size of
Seattle. Traffic jams, for instance. But that reason
didn't hold up when she considered he was supposed
to have been home hours ago. He should have checked
in with his family, had dinner with them, then left in
plenty of time to get C.J.'s call.

No, whatever had detained him was more involved
than a mere traffic jam. If he'd gotten wrapped up in
doing surveillance on someone, he might have turned
off his pager, or perhaps he'd been unable to get away.
His not being where he was supposed to be didn't
mean anything was wrong. Nor did it mean everything was all right.

With a quiet groan, she pushed the chair away from
the desk and stood. She could chase her pessimistic
thoughts in circles from now until she caught up with
Keith again, and all she'd gain from the effort was a
headache and a sleepless night. But she couldn't turn
off the fear. If something had indeed happened to
him, where would she go? Who could she trust to help
her?

Sitting in the surveillance van, Frank Matlock tuned
out Hal Jennings's endless whining about the paperwork he was neglecting while they listened in on Keith
Taylor's home phone. If the man had any brains he
would be more concerned with finding the Dillon sis-

ters. The longer they were free, the bigger the chance they might blow the lid on the network. The men at the top didn't like to lose. When they did, the guys at the bottom usually took the fall for them.

"Got something for you, maybe." The kid tracing the calls in and out of the Taylor home handed Matlock the headphones just as the call ended.

"What was it?" he growled.

"A woman. Said she was someone's secretary. I just thought it was kinda late for a secretary to be working."

Late was right. It was well after eleven o'clock. "Play it back."

Matlock listened to the recorded conversation, but there was too much static on the line to get a good make on the woman's voice. Still, as the kid had said, most offices would have closed hours ago. Odd that anyone's secretary would still be working. Matlock had learned to pay attention to inconsistencies, and this was a big one. Could this woman caller be C.J. Dillon? It was worth checking out. Especially since Taylor and Dillon had worked together.

"Did you pinpoint the call?" Matlock asked.

The kid shook his head. "Not enough time. All I could get was it came from out of the city."

Matlock smoothed down his dark mustache, working to hold on to his ever-shortening temper. C.J. Dillon had outwitted him at every turn so far.

When Jennings called two days ago to say Taylor was investigating him, Matlock had checked out the reporter. When he discovered that C.J. Dillon had once worked with Taylor, Matlock had caught the first flight to Seattle. This was the best lead they'd had on the two women and he wasn't taking any chances.

Had C.J. asked Taylor to help her find an honest FBI agent in Seattle? Was that why he was so interested in Hal Jennings? The odds were good, very good, in fact.

Matlock wanted answers. He'd gotten nothing from Taylor earlier in the evening. Nothing but more frustration and a bruised hand. Taylor was now in the hospital. According to the police scanner, his unconscious body had been found and transported to the hospital fifteen minutes ago. Word had come back that he was in critical condition with a concussion and numerous broken bones. It was uncertain whether he would recover from his injuries.

The "secretary" had said she would call back in the morning, though. Hopefully Mrs. Taylor would be willing to assist in apprehending the person responsible for his injuries. If Matlock convinced her "Mr. Wexler" was the guilty party, she would keep the "secretary" on the phone long enough that they could get a positive trace on her position. And in the meantime, he would run this Wexler's name through the computer.

Everything was finally falling into place.

Chapter 4

Annie and C.J. were finishing breakfast when Chris walked into the diner. One look at his lean, wide-shouldered frame and C.J.'s heartbeat picked up its pace. Along with her concern for Keith, the memory of Chris's kiss had haunted her well into the night. She'd been stunned and confused by her response, and tormented by an unfamiliar sense of longing.

Chris waved to Shari, then in his long stride, headed for the booth where C.J. and Annie sat. Noticing he wore tight-fitting jeans and a denim jacket instead of his uniform, C.J. tried to recall what she'd agreed to last night. All she could remember was the feel of his arms around her.

"Mornin', ladies."

His casual smile brightened when his gaze landed on C.J. The warmth reached out to her, as tangible and intimate as a caress. She wanted to lean into that warmth, to wrap it around herself like a shield. She knew she couldn't give in, yet her resistance weakened more each time he was near.

"Hi, Chris," Annie greeted him cheerfully. "C.J., move over. He doesn't want to sit next to me and my germs." She sniffled for effect.

C.J. scooted over, giving her sister a not-so-subtle kick in the shin. Annie jumped slightly, but her maddening smirk only widened as Chris squeezed into the booth.

He settled closer than necessary, C.J. thought as she worked to suppress the impulse to nestle against him. His size and nearness made her feel safe and vulnerable at the same time—a disconcerting sensation for her, and completely inappropriate under the present circumstances. Why couldn't she control her reaction to this particular man? She'd been running on fear and adrenaline for more than a week—maybe that was the reason she couldn't seem to rein in her hormones when he was around.

"Uniform at the cleaners?" Annie asked him, scooping up the last of her scrambled eggs.

"Even the sheriff gets a day off now and then." Smiling, he draped his arm over the back of the seat and leaned toward C.J. "Our horses await."

She frowned, still unable to shake the desire to settle into his embrace. His voice was deep, seductive. The fragrance of soap and his pine-scented after-shave was as alluring as when he'd held her in his arms last night.

"Horses?" she asked, struggling to bring her racing heartbeat under control.

"You're invited, too," he said, glancing at Annie.

"No, thanks. I don't go within spitting distance of any animal bigger than a cocker spaniel."

"That leaves you and me, then." He smiled at C.J.

Her heart stumbled in reaction to the heat in his gaze. It held promises of things it was safer not to give in to—passion, warmth, caring. She couldn't risk it, not now. Maybe not ever.

"I'll stay with Annie," she said.

"You agreed and I'm holding you to it."

She stiffened at his insistence. "'Mmm' is not an agreement. I couldn't concentrate on what you were saying."

"She must have had a camera in her hands when you asked," Annie put in with a chuckle. "When she's taking pictures, even an explosion won't distract her."

Chris flashed a satisfied grin. "Nope. This time she was holding me."

His voice had taken on a husky tone as he looked at C.J. Annie's surprised gaze flew to C.J.'s face. When Annie turned her bright blue eyes back to Chris, C.J. could see her sister's too-vivid imagination was already working overtime.

"A day out in the fresh air and sunshine is just what C.J. needs," she said enthusiastically. "She doesn't relax often enough."

Chris nodded. "I've gathered that."

"She's been like this for as long as I can remember. Dad always said her job was to remind us life wasn't all fun and games, and our job was to remind her life wasn't all work and responsibility."

"You and he must have had your hands full."

"Very funny, Sheriff," C.J. muttered, setting her fork on her plate and pushing it aside. She was the one who'd had her hands full, protecting her father and sister from people who deliberately tried to take advantage of their easy trust and overly generous natures.

"I'll bet she was a model teenager," Chris continued. "No staying out past curfew, no getting into trouble, no wild love affairs."

"Well, there was one guy. C.J. was pretty upset when they split up."

She'd been furious beyond words, C.J. thought. But no one would ever know how hard she'd fallen for Marty Kendall. She had trusted him completely, stupidly, had told him things about herself and her family she'd never shared with anyone else. He'd kept up the pretense of caring for her just long enough to con her father out of three thousand dollars, then he'd run off with another woman.

"Then this guy broke her heart?" Chris asked solemnly.

"Enough." C.J. held up her hand. It was time she got the conversation back on its original track before Annie became any more talkative. "Chris, are you still determined to entertain us today?"

"More than ever." He winked at Annie.

C.J. sighed, afraid she was losing the battle to maintain some distance from Chris. Somewhere along the way she'd lost control of the situation, and of her own senses. She wanted to be with him, wanted to forget the risks. But she'd done that once before and had lost. This time the consequences would be deadly. Still, she couldn't help but wish things could be different.

"Then since Annie won't ride a horse," she said, "how about a car trip instead?"

"I don't know, C.J. I'm still not fully recovered." Annie coughed and sniffled again. "You go without me."

"Fresh air and sunshine are just what you need. If you have any doubts, come upstairs and we'll discuss them while I get my camera and you get your box of tissues." C.J.'s tone left no room for protest.

"You'll need your jackets, too." Chris stood to let her out of the booth.

He towered over her—formidable and alluring at the same time. C.J. wanted to run away from him, to safety, and she desperately wanted to stay. She was having enough trouble fighting her own illogical and bewildering feelings for the sheriff without Annie's blatant attempts at romance, she thought as her sister led the way up the stairs.

Once they reached the room, Annie grabbed C.J.'s arm. "You don't want me tagging along."

C.J. fixed her with a pointed glare. "If you think I'm going to go chasing around the countryside and leave you here alone, you're crazy."

"Oh, lighten up, big sister." Annie walked over to the dresser to examine her hair in the mirror. "If Matlock hasn't shown up by now, we've lost him."

"Not necessarily." C.J. thought of Keith, wondering if he was all right, if she and Annie really were safe.

"Even if he did show up while you were out with Chris," Annie insisted, "he wouldn't do anything to me until he had the evidence, which would be with you."

C.J. set her camera bag on the bed and reached inside to check her film supply, aware that Annie's typically blasé attitude annoyed her more than usual.

"This isn't a movie script," she snapped. "You pose the most threat to him and Jordainne. You worked in the senator's campaign office in D.C. You know where the illegal contributions came from, and how they were supposed to be hidden."

"I wish I'd never gotten involved with that worm."

"Well, you did and now you have more information in your head than there is in those ledgers and the other documents you swiped from his safe."

"And I nearly got us killed. Why is it the one man we handed the evidence to had to be in with Jordainne's network?"

"He's not the only agent on that network's payroll, I'd bet. That's why Keith insisted we let him check out Jennings before we get into Seattle." C.J. looked up from her equipment long enough to frown at Annie. "And how do you know those ledgers and Jordainne's personal diary will be with me?"

"I put two and two together. You've been abnormally protective of your camera bag, so I figured there must be more in it than your equipment. Like I figure Chris doesn't want a chaperon."

"He doesn't have a choice." C.J. snatched up Annie's jacket and tossed it to her. "So you can forget any notions of romance."

"Someone has to look out for your nonexistent love life. Whenever a relationship starts to get personal, you run the other way."

"I do not."

"Yes, you do. Once a man gets romantic, you hightail it out of town so fast no one knows you're gone until they meet the people subletting your apartment."

Very annoyed at the truth in her sister's words, C.J. shoved her hands through the sleeves of her own jacket. "Now is not the time to start a relationship."

"Why not? Chris could be the best thing that ever came along for you and you'll never have this chance to find out again. Damn it, C.J., you're always so busy anticipating problems and worrying about what's going to happen tomorrow that you can't appreciate what you have today."

Hand on the camera bag strap, C.J. paused to stare as Annie's normally placid nature gave way to a rare show of exasperation and impatience.

"And while you're thinking about that," she continued, her hands planted on her small hips, "ask yourself just who you're upset with—me for noticing Chris's obvious interest in you and doing something about it, or yourself for not having the guts to take a chance."

She stalked out of the room, leaving C.J. staring after her. Annie was both intelligent and intuitive, something C.J. tended to overlook. However, her sister was also terminally optimistic and an incurable romantic.

Annie liked to take chances. C.J. took them only when the odds were stacked in her favor. Annie looked forward to surprises. C.J. didn't like to be caught in situations where the outcome was uncertain, or where she was dependent upon the whims of another person. As in romance. She'd tried that once and wasn't in a hurry to try it again.

Starting down the stairs, she decided staying alive took priority over involvement with the local sheriff, no matter how devastating his smile, or how tempting

he looked standing by the front door. Annie was nowhere in sight.

"Where—" she began cautiously.

"Talking to Shari." Chris pointed to the diner.

C.J. nodded, then headed for the office. "I have to
make a quick phone call. To an editor who may have
an assignment for me," she added, seeing the curiosity in Chris's glance.

The call to Keith's home was even quicker than she
planned. No one answered. Surprising since it was
only eight-thirty Seattle time, she thought, tensing.
She dialed the number at the newspaper. Six rings later
the phone was finally answered. Not by Keith, but by
a harried-sounding co-worker. The man told her Keith
wasn't there, but his calendar said he had an appoint-
ment at the mayor's office.

That didn't tell C.J. whether Keith was safe.
"Would you tell him Mr. Wexler's secretary called?"
she asked.

"Hang on." He rustled some papers. "Keith's wife
called this morning. She said if you phoned here to tell
you Keith's very busy working on something, and you
should call him at the house at nine tonight." Message delivered, the man hung up.

C.J. bit her lower lip. Chances were Keith was sitting across the desk from Seattle's mayor, asking
pointed questions and jotting notes in his indecipher-
able shorthand. Just as he'd most likely arrived home
hours late last night, to find his dinner cold and his
wife's shoulder even colder.

He'd probably been involved with the investigation
into Jennings and hadn't been able to get away. Maybe
that was why he'd had his wife leave that message at
the paper. Or maybe not. He was throwing their pre-

arranged timetable out the window, along with all their precautions in case someone was monitoring his phone calls—something very unlike him.

Perhaps he'd found out Jennings was on the up-and-up, and there was no longer any need for the elaborate safety measures. Still, C.J. would feel much better if she could talk to him personally.

She stood as the door opened.

"Everything all right?" Annie asked, closing the door behind her.

C.J. didn't want to upset her sister when hopefully there was nothing to worry about. She swallowed her doubts and fears and nodded.

"Good. Then maybe, in light of the things I said upstairs..."

"I'll reconsider and ride out of here with the sheriff, leaving you behind?" she finished for Annie.

"It's only for a few hours, C.J., not a lifetime."

C.J. smiled wryly. "Maybe I am worrying too much."

"And maybe you do want to be alone with him?" Annie added with a speculative gleam in her eyes.

Annie was right, C.J. decided. She did want to be with Chris. She was scared and worried, but even that was not enough to rein in her wayward hormones. With a sigh, she hugged her sister.

"What will you do while we're gone?" she asked as Annie walked her to the door.

"Visit with Shari. Help her out with the diner. Don't worry about me, even though that would be completely contrary to your nature."

C.J. made a face at her sister as she was ushered outside. Chris waited beside the car, holding the door for her. C.J. hesitated, trying to squelch the anticipation that raced through her. Undeniable longings tugged her toward him, to his strength and integrity, to his virility and vitality, to his sunny smiles and the heat of hunger in his eyes. Fear held her back, reminding her of past mistakes, and that a miscalculation now would mean certain death.

With a concerted effort, she squared her shoulders and walked toward this man who had her sense of logic thoroughly confused.

"Where's Annie?" he asked as C.J. got into the car.

"She decided to stay with Shari."

C.J. thought she spotted a satisfied grin on his face as he hoisted the camera bag into the front seat, then got in behind the wheel.

"Did you get the job?" he asked once he'd started the engine.

"Job?"

"The phone call you made. Did you get the assignment?"

C.J.'s heartbeat faltered for one moment. "Oh. He wasn't in." How could she have forgotten? Collecting her thoughts, she reached for the seat belt. She hated having to be dishonest with him, but in this situation, she had little choice. If she was going to be alone with him, she would have to be very careful about what she said.

"Where are we going?" she asked as they left the city limits.

"A spot up in the Bighorn Mountains."

Chris put the Jeep in gear, wondering if there was more to the phone call than what little she'd told him. Pulling onto a narrow winding road an hour later, he decided there probably was. C.J. had held up her end of the conversation during the drive, but he could read the subtle body language signs that said plainer than words she was upset. Her shoulders were tense, her back rigid, and unless she was answering a direct question, her mood was pensive.

Problems with the assignment? Or was there something more on her mind? The license check on the Toyota hadn't come back yet. He'd told Oliver to radio him if the paperwork came through while he was out, but it could still be tomorrow before they got anything back.

Finding out what kind of trouble C.J. was in had become more and more imperative to him. It wasn't anything he could put his finger on, just a gut instinct telling him all was not as it seemed, and that C.J. was running from something. But he doubted he would get a direct answer if he asked about it. Her habit of evading questions annoyed him and piqued his curiosity at the same time.

Time, he thought, pulling off the road and onto a flat spot in the grass, was one thing he didn't have an excess of. In a few days, she would be headed for Montana. Billings wasn't that far from Northfield, but once she left, he had the feeling he would never see her again. That thought bothered him a lot.

He shut off the engine. "Will this spot do?"

"It's gorgeous," C.J. whispered.

Looking at the lush green hills dotted with patches of straight, tall pine trees, Chris felt a touch of the same reverence he heard in her voice. It was like that every time he came up here, no matter how frequently. No two views were the same, and each one was even more incredibly breathtaking than any other.

"Interested enough to take a few pictures?" he asked.

She gave him a slow smile, one that flashed her fascinating dimple at him. "One or two."

"All right, then. Let's get the gear unloaded."

Grinning, she hopped out and walked around to the back of the Jeep. While he opened the tailgate, she set her camera bag on the ground and took a long, deep breath, then exhaled, stretching her arms high over her head. Maybe she was finally relaxing, Chris thought, trying not to be obvious as he watched her denim jacket ride up to reveal jeans that fit her trim waist and the curve of her hips.

His thoughts took a rapid detour from nature's scenery to the delectable sight in front of his eyes. She was slender, shapely, and he wanted to feel her pressed against his hard length again. He wanted even more than that. Each time he was with her the desire had grown, until now he was almost overwhelmed with a need for her. She swamped his senses, short-circuited his brain, overloaded his hormones. Would he ever get the chance to explore these feelings?

"What's there to unload except the picnic hamper?" she asked.

"This." Reluctantly Chris pulled his thoughts away from dreams of passionate lovemaking, handed her a blanket, then dug out a Frisbee.

"You're kidding?" she said, eyeing the orange disk.

"Nope. I figured we could get in a game or two before we eat." He set the picnic basket on the ground and closed the tailgate.

"Okay, cowboy." C.J. twirled the Frisbee on one finger, her blue-gray eyes mirroring the challenge in her smile. "I'll show you how the game is played."

"We'll see about that. Then after we eat," Chris said, pointing off into the distance, "I'll show you some of the sights."

They left the picnic basket and blanket a few feet from the car and walked down the small hillside to where the ground leveled off a little. Once C.J. set her camera bag out of harm's way, they drew up the boundary lines, hashed out the rules, then started the game.

She knew how to handle a Frisbee, but where he was out to have fun, C.J. played to win. Chris had to admit she gave him a workout.

Keeping up would be easier if it wasn't for his awareness of her. He'd lost the first game; the second was almost over, he was two points down and needed his concentration. But C.J. made it impossible for him to keep his mind on the game. Everything about her captured his attention—the ring of her laughter, the way her complexion glowed from the exertion.

Then, as if that wasn't enough, she'd taken off her jacket and the view was driving him to distraction. Each time she stretched to catch the Frisbee, her firm breasts strained against her checkered blouse. He wanted to hold her in his arms again, to sample more of the fire of her kiss, to taste all of her passion.

He caught the Frisbee, then tossed it back, half glad, half frustrated when a gust of wind lifted it high into the air and C.J. ran backward, determined to catch it. Another stab of longing hit him full force as she jumped and reached. Chris watched her graceful ascent, so totally absorbed with the allure of her gently curved figure, he barely noticed the disk soar above her outstretched fingertips.

"That's out of boun—" Her jubilant shout ended abruptly as she came down on her right foot. Her heel slid out from under her. She hit the ground with a thud Chris heard from his end of the playing field. She didn't move, didn't groan. He couldn't tell if she was even breathing. His own breath trapped in his lungs, he raced over to where she lay flat on the ground.

He knelt beside her, his heart pounding. "C.J.?"

"That's game...point," she whispered breathlessly.

Chris wanted to shout to hell with the game. "So you won," he snapped, "but are you going to live to tell about it?"

"Just...bruised," C.J. said, still struggling to get her breath.

She raised up on one elbow and groaned. Chris slipped an arm around her waist to help her sit, then sat beside her, supporting her back with his chest.

"Sure nothing's broken?" he asked gently.

C.J. nodded, afraid her voice would betray the emotions and sensations his nearness created. How could such a tiny, innocent amount of physical contact catapult her into chaos? She shouldn't crave his caring and concern, shouldn't melt at his gentle touch, shouldn't ache for more. But she did and the feelings were stronger than any she'd ever experienced. She'd spent her whole life taking care of others. Why should this one man make her long to be taken care of? She breathed heavily to banish the thoughts, but they wouldn't budge.

He let out a relieved sigh. "Then I officially declare the game over and it's time to investigate the food."

"Who put you in charge?" C.J. asked good-naturedly, her voice sounding a little stronger.

"Now I'm sure you'll live. You scared the hell out of me, though," Chris scolded lightly, holding her close.

"My tailbone will never be the same."

"Can you move your legs?"

C.J. did, wincing as she bent one leg, then the other. Her movements were slow and careful. The heat of him warmed her back, making her languid, content to rest in his embrace. With a concerted effort she forced the illogical thoughts and wishes aside.

"Sore, but nothing broken or dislocated," she assured him, not wanting to put distance between them, but knowing she had to. "If you'll just help me up..."

After seeing her hit the ground the way she had, Chris wasn't sure he could stand himself. He took a moment to catch his breath, then got shakily to his feet.

"Put your hands on my arms and let me do the work." Bending over her, he put one hand on either side of her small waist. She groaned again as he carefully pulled her up. Once she was standing, he held her against his chest, steadying her. "Doing okay?"

C.J. nodded. "Just give me a minute." She wasn't ready to give up all contact just yet. What would a few more moments in his arms hurt? Soon enough she would leave, go back to the uncertainty of running. She would never again feel this secure, this treasured. Was it wrong to want the moment to last a little longer?

"Take as long as you like."

They could stand this way for a very long time, Chris thought, loving the feel of her softness pressed against him. She fit nicely, snugly, next to him. He rested his chin lightly on her head. Her delicate scent drifted up to tease his nostrils. He ran a hand lightly over her soft hair, letting the curls wrap around his thick fingers the way he had imagined all night.

"Did you hit your head when you fell?" he asked.

"Nope."

She said the word in the same tone and with the same inflection he generally used, he noticed. Glancing down at her upturned face, he caught her mischievous smile and grinned back.

He picked a blade of grass out of a silky chestnut ringlet. "Smart mouth."

"Right now another part of my anatomy smarts more." Her voice trembled. He was so close, so tempting, making her want things she shouldn't. C.J. didn't understand what he was doing to her senses, but she knew she needed some distance. "Maybe you should walk me around a bit."

"I have a better idea."

She felt so right in his arms, a contradictory mixture of fragility and strength. The angle of her chin declared her invincibility, yet on the rare occasions she let down her guard, he'd seen the vulnerability in her eyes. Like now. Like last night just before she'd given herself up to his kiss.

He bent his head and lowered his mouth to hers, drinking in the taste of her, drowning in the feel of her, caught up in the needs and longings he'd held in check all morning. All night, too. He'd never known anyone like her. She unleashed his desire to ravish and cherish, to plunder and protect, to take and to give. She had his head reeling with the conflicting wants and emotions churning inside him.

For one crazy moment as his lips met hers, the wind ceased to blow, the birds were silent, the clouds halted in their path across the sky. C.J. felt her world come to a stop, then lurch as it suddenly spun on its axis. She wrapped her arms around Chris's waist, clinging to him for support against the tempest raging within her.

Flames of heat engulfed her, yet she shivered. Sensations ricocheted and exploded inside her, yet she'd never felt more alive, more whole. Nothing had ever been so right.

The passion within his kiss was tempered with gentleness, as though he was afraid of hurting her. His caring cast a spell of its own, one that held her bound to him as surely as his strong arms held her his willing prisoner. She gave, too stunned by her own reactions to think of holding back. She melted into his embrace, loving the heat of his hands on her shoulders, on her back, in her hair. She opened her mouth to his tender exploration. The stroke of his tongue lit a fire on her lower lip, at the corners of her mouth, deep inside.

She moved her hands up the hard plane of his back, delighting in the feel of the muscles that tensed under her touch. His hold on her tightened. One hand on the small of her back and the other lost in her hair, he pressed her closer to him. C.J. stirred in his arms, the aching need making her restless, anxious for more. Moaning, Chris abruptly pulled his mouth from hers.

He sighed, resting his chin on the top of her head once more. "We're a hell of a combination, aren't we?"

When she stiffened in his arms, Chris pulled away enough so he could look into her eyes. They were large, darkened with passion and clouded with uncertainty.

"I don't think—" she began. Her voice was unsteady, barely a whisper.

He pressed his fingertips to her lips to silence her protest. "If you're about to say this isn't a good idea, you can save your breath."

Her chin raised a determined notch. "I don't have casual affairs—"

"There's nothing casual about the way I feel when I hold you." He caught a curl of her wind-tousled hair and tucked it behind her ear, savoring the softness of her skin against his fingers. "I won't push you, C.J."

The husky tone in his voice as he said her name destroyed the little resolve she'd managed to summon. She couldn't run from his dangerous caring, from his mesmerizing tenderness, though she knew that relaxing her guard around him could bring disaster down on her. And Annie.

"But it's only fair to warn you in advance that I can be very persuasive, and even more persistent." His cocky half smile lifted one corner of his mouth.

C.J. felt the warmth of his grin steal over her, making her crazy with longing. She shook her head to clear her mind. "You? Persistent? Who would ever guess it?"

He slid his arm around her waist, holding her against his side. "Let's go check out the food." He bent to pick up the Frisbee, then pointed to the camera bag. "This time I'll carry the baby."

The documents... They were well hidden under the lining. Still...

C.J. started to argue, but one stiff step convinced her she wouldn't make it up the hill carrying her weight in camera equipment. Holding on to his arm for the support she would have refused from anyone else, she limped over to where the bag lay. Chris picked up her jacket and handed it to her. She slipped it on, missing his warmth as he let go of her.

She watched him bend over the bag. "Let me make sure everything's inside and it's zipped shut."

"No need, mother hen. All the little chicks are tucked safely inside." He put the strap over his shoulder. Inclining his head toward the bag, he made a little clucking sound. "Hear the little darlings?"

"Good thing you chose peacekeeping over chicken ranching. Baby chicks cheep, not cluck."

He shrugged. "Minor technicality."

"Not to the chickens."

Laughing, she linked her arm through his. She held on to him for support only, she told herself. Necessary since her sore tailbone protested every movement as they walked up the hill. But she couldn't deny it felt good to be this close to him, warm, happy, enjoying the moment, putting the fear aside for just a while. Soon enough she would have to deal with the problems chasing her.

She sighed as they topped the hill and headed for the blanket. She sat down carefully.

"What does C.J. stand for?" he asked, opening the hamper.

"I won't reveal what the *C* stands for, not even if you torture me."

He chuckled. "That bad, huh? How about the *J?*"

"Jane."

He took out a plate of fried chicken, a container of potato salad, grapes, apples, celery and carrot sticks, slices of cheese and a box of crackers.

Taking in the sight of that much food, C.J.'s eyes widened. "Where did all this come from?"

"Shari contributed the chicken and potato salad. The rest I had packed to carry in saddlebags. I stuck them in the hamper while you got your jacket and equipment."

C.J. helped herself to the fruit and cheese. "Annie doesn't realize the feast she missed out on."

Chris reached for a piece of chicken. "I think she got the idea I wanted you to myself."

"Mmm. And she was only too happy to oblige you."

"You two seem to get along with each other," he mused, reaching for some of the cheese.

"Only when we're apart," C.J. said, smiling at the bemused and bewildered expression in his green eyes. "Didn't you fight with your brothers or sisters?"

"Didn't have any," he said very matter-of-factly. "I was raised in foster homes. There were other kids, but none of us were related, and none of us were very friendly."

Not an easy childhood, C.J. thought at the rare lack of expression in his voice. Little laughter, less warmth and no love. Yet he'd managed to evolve into a caring and responsible man. She longed to know about that journey, about his transformation and how it had happened. But she couldn't afford to get any closer.

"Well, let me tell you," she said with an exaggerated sigh, "you didn't miss out on a thing not having a younger sister as stubborn as Annie."

Chris laughed. "Do you travel a lot with her?"

Shaking her head, C.J. dabbed the corners of her mouth with a napkin. "She's a homebody. As soon as she graduated from high school, she came to D.C., hoping after all the traveling by myself, I would decide to settle down.''

Chris frowned, training an intent gaze on C.J., wondering again about the New York plates on her car and what the license check would show.

Her stories weren't adding up. She was having so much trouble keeping them straight—obviously she didn't lie often. Someone with more practice at deceit wouldn't make the mistakes she'd made. If only he could find some way to make her realize he would be on her side, that it was safe to talk to him. But how?

"If you're from Nebraska, and she came to D.C. after high school," he said slowly, carefully, "where does New York fit in?"

"New York?" C.J. asked weakly.

"The other day you told me she'd moved from New York to D.C."

C.J. jerked so suddenly she would have overturned the jug of lemonade if Chris hadn't reached out to steady it. "She had some idea of attending NYU," she said hastily, standing and reaching for the camera bag.

"What about lunch?" Chris asked her, his brow knit. Something was definitely wrong, and he wanted to get to the bottom of the matter. Now. Not when she was ready to tell him.

If he pushed, though, C.J. would clam up altogether. She might even flee. She was resourceful enough to find a way. At least here, he could protect her if need be. He would have to let the issue of the license plates slide for the time being. Concentrate on gaining her trust, getting her to open up. But, damn, it was frustrating to wait.

"I want to get some shots while there's light," she said.

"Okay. There's a spot not far from here I want to show you." He took the camera bag from her hand before she could object, then pocketed an apple.

Those damn stolen license plates, C.J. thought, starting down the hill with Chris beside her. The conversation kept coming back to them. She'd allayed his suspicions once before, but what about this time? Did he believe her? As they walked, she was conscious of his eyes on her. She knew he sensed her nervousness, and tried to cover it with questions.

But it wasn't easy. Between Keith's unavailability and having to watch every word she or Annie said, she had more on her mind than she could juggle. Then add to that her attraction to the man at her side. She was drawn to him and, despite the dangers that presented, she couldn't fight it.

"Do you live in Northfield?" she asked when they came to a narrow stream that rushed over a bed of rocks. She knelt down and rifled the bag for a wide-angle lens.

"About halfway between there and Redman. I have a log house I built."

That would suit him, she thought, imagining solid construction, rough-hewn beams and open rooms. "What do you do in the winter? Besides shovel snow, I mean."

She took meter readings and checked the settings on the Nikon while he detailed his activities from Wednesday-night poker games, to hunting and fishing trips, to rescuing stranded motorists during blizzards. All the while, his intent gaze remained on her, watching her thoughtfully.

If only she had a clue as to what he was thinking. Did he accept the story that Annie had wanted to try

NYU, and the earlier tale that she hadn't yet registered the car in D.C.? If he didn't, she and Annie would have a hell of a time handling the trouble he would cause them. They wouldn't be able to explain their way out of jail.

She threw out more questions with each frame she shot, not giving him a chance to ask any of his own. If she didn't have to answer, she wouldn't have to lie. The two lies she'd already told were creating enough problems.

Adjusting the shutter speed to compensate for the clouds rolling in, she sighed. Her common sense hadn't been particularly strong in the face of the desire Chris brought to life in her. He was pure sex appeal wrapped up in a ruggedly male package that made it impossible for her to control her awareness. She should be doing everything she could to avoid him. Instead she was wanting him more than she'd ever wanted a man. And the very traits she admired in him could present major complications for her should he find out she and Annie were wanted by the law he'd sworn to uphold. He would be formidable in a confrontation. C.J. didn't want to dwell on that frightening thought.

She crossed the stream to shoot it from another angle, for once more concerned with his answers to the steady questions she threw at him than with her subject.

His love of the area was obvious. She saw it in his eyes as he pointed out the tiny waterfall tucked between the two hills on either side of them. She heard it in his voice as he described the beauty of the changing seasons, the challenge of the rugged winters, the wealth of natural wonders to be found and the indomitable spirit of the people living in the region.

She envied the sense of belonging he had. Even in Mason Falls she'd never felt really comfortable, completely a part of the place and the people. She sat back on her heels and rewound the film in the camera.

Chris watched her, wondering what was going through her mind. Some of her earlier tension had ebbed away, but she was definitely still on guard. He didn't like going behind her back to find out what she was running from, but she left him little choice. When he got back to the office, he would see what had turned up on the Toyota's ID number.

Her unwillingness to confide in him made Chris angry, though he understood her fear of strangers. He wanted her to trust him. But he had the uneasy feeling she might wait until it was too late. Gut instinct said she might be in over her head.

"Are you packing up?" he asked as she opened the camera and put in a fresh roll of film.

"I'm losing the light." She dropped the used canister back into the film box and marked it with the letters *WY.*

"Which is our cue to head back." He slung the camera bag's strap over his shoulder.

C.J. didn't object, though she was recovered enough to manage the equipment on her own now. It seemed so natural to let him carry it for her. Something was happening between them, something she didn't understand, didn't want to acknowledge, couldn't ignore. A startling shift in her priorities had occurred somewhere along the line. A shift she couldn't afford, but couldn't do anything about.

For the first time she noticed the briskness of the breeze. She shoved her hands in her jacket pockets. Other parts of the country would be enjoying balmy temperatures, while the people here were preparing for winter.

Being in northern Wyoming in late September could work to her advantage, she hoped. A region where the weather could turn treacherous with little warning might be one of the last places Matlock would look for his quarry. But he wasn't an amateur at tracking people who didn't want to be found.

She couldn't afford to get snowed in while he narrowed down the list of possible places they might hide. Again she was hit with the sense of urgency that had pushed her across the country. This time, though, the feeling was accompanied by a definite reluctance to leave.

"You're very quiet all of a sudden," Chris commented as they came out on the other side of the trees.

C.J. smiled ruefully. She'd quizzed him for details on just about every phase of his life in Wyoming, and every answer he'd given had led to another question. "Figured I've driven you crazy with my curiosity."

"I don't mind it, coming from you."

He draped an arm around her shoulders. It felt so natural to walk that way with him. Without pausing to analyze the feeling, she slipped her arm around his waist. For these few moments, she didn't want to think, to worry, just enjoy the peace and comfort of being near him. Too soon she would be on her own again. This time, she wasn't looking forward to it.

When they reached the top of the hill, they repacked the picnic remains and stowed them in the back of the Jeep. Chris put the camera bag on the floor of

the front seat and held the door while C.J. got in. He
checked to make sure the tailgate was locked, then got
in behind the steering wheel.

With every passing mile, C.J. yearned for more time
here, with him. Fear, she thought, attempting to ra-
tionalize her uncharacteristic desire to lean on someone, to stay with someone for an extended period of
time. Fear of what she and Annie would face once
they were on the road again. Fear of Matlock finding
them. Chris was a safe haven. There'd been too few of
those in C.J.'s life. But he was danger, as well, a fact
she tended to forget too easily.

The graying clouds mirrored her darkening thoughts
as they pulled up in front of the hotel. She should be
in a hurry to leave, to run to the safety of the hotel
room. Instead she felt an undeniable pull to remain
with Chris, a longing to be wrapped in his warm embrace and kept safe from the demons following her.
But trust was such a risky business, and this time her
very life hung in the balance, hers and Annie's.

Chris opened her door, pleased to note no one was
around. He'd hoped they could have a few more moments alone. He didn't want to let her go without
kissing her once more, without holding her in his arms
for a while. He laid his hands on her shoulders. His
eyes caressed the contours of her face.

C.J. sensed what was to come, but she couldn't
make herself pull away. His gaze lingered on her
mouth, then he bent his head. She braced, preparing
for the shock waves that swamped her senses each time
his mouth touched hers, the warmth and the rush of
excitement that poured through her when he held her.
She closed her eyes, savoring the woodsy scent of him,

the strength in his arms, the hardness of his body, the gentle firmness of his mouth.

She was sinking deeper under the waves of longing that surrounded her, aching, yearning for more. Then slowly he pulled away, cradling her head against his chest. His heart beat a racing rhythm under her ear.

Until now no one had, with just one kiss, one look, made her body come so alive. Would she ever feel this way with any other man? Somehow she sensed the memories of her few moments with him might have to last her a very long time.

"You make it awfully hard to keep my promise not to push," he said softly against her ear.

"But you're a man of your word, aren't you?"

Chris heard the note of regret in her question. She was afraid, still not convinced she could trust him. She needed time. He understood that. But how much time did they have? He would never be able to stand by and watch her leave, knowing she was in trouble. He was sorely tempted to lock her up and throw away the key, anything to get her to tell him what was going on.

He studied her expression, reading fear and uncertainty in the blue-gray depths of her eyes. He wanted to shake her in frustration, to force her to tell him what she was running from. But he didn't have that right, personally or professionally. He had no claim on her affections or her loyalty, and his gut instinct told him she'd committed no crime. However, he was determined to know what she was hiding from him. Her safety was that important to him, and he wasn't going to question why.

"I'll keep my word," he said, deciding he would stick as close to her as possible. "You, however, have to give me a chance to try out my powers of persuasion."

That meant spending more time with him, C.J. thought with alarm. She longed to tell him she would give him anything he wanted, everything he asked for. How unbelievably wonderful it would be to give her emotions free rein, to lose control and know that he would take care of her. But these were feelings she couldn't entertain. No matter how badly she wanted to confide her secrets to him, she didn't dare.

"I need to get inside," she said, pulling away from him, away from his strength, away from the potential danger he represented. He let her go without a fight. This time. But what would happen the next time?

With a mixture of anticipation and trepidation, C.J. watched him get into the Jeep and drive away. She climbed the stairs to her room, telling herself again she should be relieved that she and Annie would soon be back on the road to Seattle. But all she felt was empty, weary to the bone.

"A girl who's just been kissed by the sexiest man in Wyoming ought to look a little happier about it," Annie commented as C.J. walked in the room.

"How...?"

"I was looking out the window," Annie supplied with a sly grin.

Sighing wearily, C.J. dropped her jacket on the foot of her bed and sat down to untie her shoes.

"Mike came by and said he found an engine," Annie told her. "He'll be able to start on the car tomorrow morning."

Where was the surge of elation she should have felt? C.J. wondered. Two days and he would have the Toyota running. But all she could think about was she'd be leaving Redman, and Chris.

Annie caught her arm as she stood. "C.J., I've been thinking. Sit down." She moved over to make room on the narrow bed. "Couldn't we turn the evidence over to Chris?"

C.J. shook her head.

"Why not? He's a lawman. One we can trust."

"He'll arrest us."

"No. He would believe us. Wouldn't he?"

C.J. gazed into her sister's plaintive eyes and shook her head again. Annie was grasping at any means to put an end to the running, but she hadn't looked at it from the reverse angle. Chris might have the potential to solve their problems, but he might also spell disaster for them.

"He may be inclined to believe us," C.J. said carefully, not wanting to raise Annie's hopes. "But he doesn't know the first thing about us. Our story will sound preposterous on the surface—an FBI agent in league with known criminals, and the distinguished senator from Pennsylvania, the man being groomed for the presidency a few years down the road, taking bribes and illegal campaign contributions, and laundering money for men under indictment for nearly every type of criminal activity imaginable—"

"But it's true. We have the evidence."

"And evidence can be manufactured."

Annie's eyes widened. "But we wouldn't..."

"Chris doesn't know that. Not for sure. And until he was completely certain, his duty would come first. He would have to detain us while he sorted through the facts."

"Would that be so bad? We'd be under his protection."

"Think about it. He would check with the FBI and Matlock would come running. Whatever charges he's trumped up against us will be damn convincing. Why should Chris take our word over that of a fellow lawman?"

"He couldn't believe that snake," Annie protested weakly.

"Matlock and Jordainne have fooled a lot of people. Jordainne is the All-American man. Decorated war hero. Injured in the line of duty. He's cultivated that image, right down to his limp. And Matlock's record in law enforcement is no less impressive."

"But Chris knows us—"

C.J. sighed wearily. "We've spent a day and a half with him. He knows you're in college and I'm a photographer, period. He might like us, but that doesn't mean he'll automatically take our word, and it won't keep him from doing his duty. That's the kind of man he is."

"You don't know that for sure."

"I'm not willing to stake our lives on my being wrong." She held up a hand as Annie opened her mouth. "There's something else to consider. What's to keep Matlock from killing Chris if he does believe us and refuses to turn us over?"

Annie's eyes widened even more as she absorbed the shocking thought. "What about the FBI man in Seattle?"

"Jennings?"

"Yeah. If Keith says this man is honest, he's going to detain us, too. What's to keep Matlock from killing him, too? I think we'd be better off right where we are.''

C.J. realized how badly Annie wanted to stay. Redman had been their sanctuary for a few days and she didn't want to leave. But she had to face the fact that the longer they stayed in one place, the more dangerous it was for them.

"Seattle isn't as isolated as Redman," C.J. pointed out patiently. "The FBI building will be full of people. It'll be too risky for Matlock to try anything. But here, I doubt there would be more than one man on duty in Chris's office. Matlock could walk in, blow us all away and be gone before anyone knew what happened.''

Annie shuddered. "Then what are we going to do?"

"Stick to our original plan and head for Seattle. By the time we get there, Keith should have something solid to tell us about Jennings." C.J. got tiredly to her feet. "Want to go down to dinner?"

Annie shook her head. "I'm not hungry. You're sure Chris would arrest us?"

C.J. gave her sister a sad smile. "I'd bet every piece of my camera equipment on it.''

And, C.J. admitted to herself, she cared enough about Chris to be concerned for his safety. She didn't doubt he could handle himself in most any situation, but Matlock and his men were ruthless. If she were responsible for something happening to Chris, she would never forgive herself.

The diner was closed when C.J. went downstairs shortly before ten. All the lights were out except for the one in the lobby. She walked behind the registration desk and into Shari's office, hoping Keith would be home and would have some good news for her. He was the one who'd set up the calls to the random pay phones, because modern technology made listening in to private conversations too easy. He'd broken the rules and C.J. could only pray it was because he'd found out it was safe to talk to Jennings.

If not, he surely would tell her so. She would hang up before a positive trace could be made and they would go back to their prearranged schedule. But the way he'd missed her other calls, then had left messages with his wife, C.J. had to know what was going on.

She reached for the phone and dialed Keith's number. Mrs. Taylor answered.

"Is Keith there?" C.J. asked.

"Who's calling, please?"

His wife still sounded upset and angry, C.J. thought, breathing in relief that she would soon be talking to Keith. When this ordeal was over, she would have to make it up to his wife for the time he'd spent helping her. "This is Mr. Wexler's secretary."

There was the slightest of pauses before Mrs. Taylor replied. Her voice sounded sharper, colder, almost bitter. "Yes, you called last night, didn't you? Can you leave a number?"

"A number?" C.J. asked, puzzling over the sudden urgency in the other woman's voice. "Isn't he there?"

"He asked me to take a number where he can reach you."

That didn't sound like Keith at all, to ask for her number. Surely he trusted his wife, but ... "I can't do that. I'll call tomorrow."

"Wait! My husband is, uh, in the hospital."

C.J.'s hand tightened on the receiver. She had to force herself to breathe normally and speak calmly through the panic choking her. Keith was hurt. "What happened?"

"An, uh, accident. He was driving home in the fog last night and he, uh, hit a telephone pole."

Easy, C.J. cautioned herself. Accidents were commonplace. Just because Matlock had engineered her accident didn't mean Keith's had been planned, too. But the coincidence stunk. "Is that what he said happened?"

"Yes. I'll see him in the morning. If you'll tell me where you're calling from, I'll ask him to—"

"That's not necessary. Which hospital is he in? I'll call him there." She had to talk to Keith personally, to hear the facts he might not be telling his wife.

"He's not allowed to receive phone calls yet. If you'll give me a message, I'll pass it on to him."

Not allowed to receive calls. That meant his injuries weren't minor. C.J. felt the warning hairs on the back of her neck prickle. "How serious is his condition?"

Mrs. Taylor cleared her throat. "He's stable. The doctors want him to rest, and Keith's such a workaholic they think it's best that he not have a telephone or visitors for a few days."

"I see. Thank you." C.J. hung up, chewing her lower lip pensively. Something was wrong with this picture. Nothing she could actually pinpoint, just a strong hunch supplied by her innate suspiciousness. This wasn't like Keith at all. But then, if he was in the hospital and not allowed phone calls, perhaps he would go through his wife to leave a message for her.

Mrs. Taylor never had answered her question as to which hospital Keith was in. C.J. had no way to track him down, not without a Seattle phone directory. There could be a dozen or more hospitals in the area. Even if she did get lucky and find out where he'd been admitted, the operator wouldn't be able to tell her more than what the doctors listed his condition as. If it was true he didn't have access to a phone, she wouldn't be able to talk to him personally. It appeared that all she could do for the moment was wait.

Jennings stepped out of the van and gave the thumbs-up sign. Looking out the Taylors' living room window, Matlock nodded.

"You did just fine, Mrs. Taylor," he said, turning to see the woman run a hand through her light brown hair.

"The bitch sounded so cool when I told her Keith was in the hospital. You'd think she didn't have a clue as to what her boss did to him. Did your man get a fix on her?"

"We got a number. We'll run it through the phone company and find her."

"And her boss, this Wexler? I want him to pay for what he did to my husband. If Keith dies..." Her hands were balled into fists at her side.

"We'll get them both, Mrs. Taylor. You can rest assured of that." Matlock let himself out the front door, smiling for the first time in ten days.

Manipulating Glenda Taylor had been as easy as he'd figured. She would never know the truth because Taylor wasn't expected to regain consciousness.

His smile widening, Matlock massaged his bruised hand. He'd told Taylor's wife he'd injured it fighting off her husband's attackers. He'd been cruising the area, he'd said, and had stumbled on to the men assaulting her husband. Before Taylor had blacked out, he'd named Wexler as the man responsible.

She'd believed every word, agreed to the tap on her phone and had kept the woman caller on the line long enough to get a positive trace.

He wasn't certain "Wexler's secretary" was C. J. Dillon, but his gut feeling said they were one and the same. Very soon he would know for sure.

Chapter 5

Her teeth worrying her lower lip, C.J. paced the workroom of Mike's garage. The mechanic and his teenage son tinkered with the rebuilt engine, thoroughly checking it out before they would place it in the rusty car. She barely noticed the smell of grease and gasoline.

For nearly an hour after the phone call to the Taylor home last night, she'd worn a path in the hardwood floor of Shari's office, trying to sort out the inconsistencies in Mrs. Taylor's voice and words. When she'd finally gone back upstairs, Annie had been sleeping soundly, fortunately, since seeing C.J. upset would panic her. Before C.J. could present the situation to her sister, she needed answers. But nearly twelve hours later, they still eluded her.

First was Keith's "accident." Was it genuine, or had it been orchestrated by Matlock or Jennings? How serious *was* his condition? Had his wife lied to her?

Possible. She'd been cold, brusque, angry. C.J. had felt as if those emotions had been directed at her specifically.

Annie frequently accused C.J. of reading much more than was meant into a tone of voice, a choice of words. She conveniently overlooked the fact that C.J. was right more often than wrong, and that her perceptions had often prevented someone's taking advantage of their father's, and Annie's, trusting, generous natures.

C.J. reached the garage doorway and did an about-face toward the back wall. Was she being paranoid now? Or had Matlock discovered her connection to Keith? She had nothing to go on, only a bunch of coincidences that seemed too convenient, and her innate nature to anticipate the worst.

She halted in mid-stride, again wondering if Matlock *had* been behind Keith's accident and had tapped the Taylors' phone. She'd been so concerned with Keith's condition and his wife's puzzling manner that she'd stayed on the line much longer than was wise.

Matlock had access to sophisticated tracing equipment. Still, if he had been listening in on the conversation, why hadn't he shown up in Redman by now? Most of the night C.J. had tried to second-guess the man. Where was he? Was his team of trained hunters closing in on her?

Pushing her hair back, she paced to the end of the workroom, turned, took another step and came face to dark green shirtfront with Chris Riker. Her mouth opened in surprise.

"Didn't mean to startle you," he said. "Guess you were more lost in thought than I realized."

He studied her expression with a mixture of thoughtful scrutiny and male appreciation that, despite her fears, brought her senses to sudden alertness. She wanted to run to him, to throw her arms around his wide solid chest, to beg him to protect her. But she couldn't do any of that. Too much was at stake to give in to these unfamiliar and puzzling emotions. Not without giving her actions a lot of thought first.

She let out a quiet breath, forcing herself to appear relaxed under his questioning gaze. What was he thinking? The color of his shirt matched the deep green of his eyes, but that was all those eyes gave away.

"How long have you been here, Sheriff?"

"Long enough to gas up the Jeep and watch you wear that groove in the concrete. Something wrong?"

His voice was quiet, full of a concern she couldn't allow herself to accept. She rapidly searched for an explanation he could accept easily.

"No offense to Redman," she said, forcing a smile, "but I'm not making any progress in my career stuck here."

"Well, ma'am, I have just the thing to take your mind off your predicament for a while." He angled his head toward the mechanics. "Mike, I left cash on the register for gas. Want me to get this restless lady out of your hair?"

Mike's answer was a grunt, but it was most definitely an affirmative. Chris took her arm and tugged his reluctant charge outside into the sunshine. His Jeep was parked in front of the pumps. Annie was settled in the back seat.

He'd planned another trip, this time without giving her any chance to back out. C.J. muttered an elo-

quent curse under her breath. With her worries over
what had happened in Seattle, she'd forgotten his
mention of horseback riding today, and his promise to
pull out all the stops to...

She felt an adrenaline rush, like the excitement and
danger involved in shooting a subject covertly. She
glanced back at the Toyota, feeling pulled in two directions. She very badly wanted to go with him, just
how badly she wanted to startled her. But she had responsibilities.

"Mike will work a lot faster without an agitated
audience," Chris stated, persistently tugging her forward.

He was right, she knew, but she was afraid. Hal
Jennings might well be working with Matlock, either
on the take along with him and Jordainne, or simply
helping out another lawman, accepting Matlock's
claims without question.

If Matlock had made her connection to Keith and
discovered he'd been checking into Jennings's past,
Matlock would put two and two together and guess
C.J. intended to run to Seattle. He might be waiting
for her when she rolled in. Keith was unavailable. She
didn't dare place another call to him, and she didn't
know where else to turn.

Perhaps it would be better to go along with Chris,
she thought as they got in the car, better if she and
Annie were away from the hotel should Matlock come
inquiring. Being with Chris might give them a small
measure of safety, the only bit available to them right
now. She would be wise to grab at that. Then, too, if
she used her time with him wisely, perhaps she could
gain more of his trust. He was in a position to pro-

vide help, as well as a measure of protection. If he was inclined to believe her.

So she gave in, joining in the conversation as rows of pine trees and tall hills whooshed by the car windows, for once struck by the magnificence of scenery created by a power greater than man. She'd never completely appreciated the intrigue of nature's haphazard blend of line and color. After growing up in rural Nebraska, she'd turned to the artfully engineered appearances of big cities, straight lines, sharp angles, cut-and-dried shades. Without her realizing it, her interest had now come full circle.

Chris turned onto a rocky road that wound up a hill and stopped in front of a small stone house. Stepping out of the car, C.J. strained for sounds of another vehicle. All she heard was the whistle of the wind through pine needles.

Then he was beside her, his hand warm on the small of her back, his gaze warmer still. She could lose herself in that look, in his softly crooked smile, in the virility emanating from him.

Catching sight of Annie's knowing smile, she pulled her stray thoughts back into line. They didn't go willingly. Even as she watched a gangly middle-aged man approach, she couldn't get Chris and his nearness off her mind.

A devilish glint lurked in his smile as he introduced Bill Hawks and asked him, "Everything set up?"

"Over there." Bill inclined his graying head toward a stable several yards away. Tethered in front of it were two horses, saddled and ready to go.

"Horses?" C.J. turned to her sister. "Don't tell me you've changed your mind—"

"Absolutely not," Annie said firmly. "You and Chris and the horses are on your own for the day. I'm going to play with little children and puppies."

C.J. wasn't sure the separation from Annie was wise, but there was nothing she could say without giving away their predicament. Besides, this might be the last time she'd have with Chris, and she was more than glad to be alone with him.

"Sara's looking forward to the company," Bill supplied. "And the help with the grandkids. Much as she loves them, they're always a handful."

"In that case, I'll go on up to the house."

Annie left, smiling blithely, leaving C.J. to wonder at the wisdom of this arrangement. Maybe she should have told Annie about Keith's accident, that she feared danger could descend on them at any moment. But then Annie would have panicked and run to Chris and damn the consequences.

If only things could be as simplistic as Annie wanted them to be. If only there was no need for precautions and contingency plans, no need to be wary of everyone. If only C.J. could take a chance on asking for Chris's help. But an error in judgment on her part could cost them their lives.

She turned to him. "Will she be all right?"

"She assured me at the hotel she felt fine, and she brought her medicine so she can take it on schedule."

There wasn't a thing C.J. could do about the situation, nothing short of spilling everything to Chris, and she needed some time to think that through. Still, she was very concerned about Annie's safety apart from her and Chris. She looked back at the house.

"You baby her too much," Chris said, bending close to speak in her ear as he turned her toward the stable.

"She'll have lots of company," Bill assured C.J. "You two just go and enjoy the fine weather. Rain's suppose to move in tonight."

C.J. paused as they neared the waiting animals. "What about my equipment?" She wasn't letting that camera bag out of her sight under any circumstances.

"Got that all planned out," Chris informed her.

And he did, C.J. thought as they rode up the hill to a narrow path through the trees a few minutes later. He'd put the camera, film and carrying bag into her saddlebags, and carefully packed the various lenses and filters into his. They had a picnic lunch so they could stay out all day. He'd also left a two-way radio with Bill and had another packed with his gear in case Annie needed C.J. or someone at the sheriff's office called for him.

Every detail had been taken care of. If only C.J. could relax and enjoy the day. The scenery was powerful, riotous, free. The sun was warm on her back, and the company, the most enjoyable, and sexiest, she'd ever known.

She wanted nothing more than to give herself up to the thrill of being with Chris. He was all the things that were so rare in the people she generally met. True hero material. He had an engaging enthusiasm for everything. His resonant laughter came easily, and each time C.J. was caught up in the sound.

Caught up in every single thing about him, she realized while giving him a lesson on photographing scenery. There was a pull on her senses, being with him, a pull on her emotions. It would be so good to linger here with him, to rest for a short while. In this place, with this man, she felt a calm that had eluded her most of her life.

Experience had taught her the feeling wouldn't last, but she wanted to stay with Chris until it was gone. Each time she showed him how to adjust the shutter speed or focus, she had to fight back the urge to lean into him, to lean on him. It seemed she'd been running for so long and now she wanted to stop.

If only she knew for sure that he would believe her story about a crooked FBI agent and the country's favorite senator, would believe the two men were connected with known criminals . . .

She sat back on her heels and sighed as her worries returned. She was so damned tired of worrying.

"Not learning fast enough for you?" He swung around and snapped a shot of her.

C.J. smiled. "You're doing great for the first time, but when you go from shooting a bird in the distance and in the shade to me nearby and in the sun, you've got to readjust all the settings."

He muttered a soft, "Damn," and shook his head. "How the hell do you do it so fast? You change them all and have a dozen frames within a heartbeat."

She chuckled as he pointed the camera at her and painstakingly adjusted the focus. Everything about him was so alluring—his enthusiasm, his boyish eagerness to learn photography, the way he lived each and every moment to the fullest. He met people with anticipation, not wariness, with warmth instead of cool reserve.

How would it be to approach life with some of his openness and not have unscrupulous people take advantage of you? Chris was not gullible in the least, not like Annie or Andrew Dillon. Anyone who tried to take advantage of the good-natured sheriff would find himself on the short end, she sensed, laughing when he snapped the picture.

He looked from her to the camera and back again. "Okay, what did I forget?"

"The shutter speed."

He growled as he studied the settings. "Because I went from shade to bright light. And the brighter the light, the faster the shutter speed, right?"

"See, you're learning."

"Then why the heavy sigh a moment ago? No, don't move," he ordered as she shifted uneasily. "I want to get this one right." He raised the camera, pressed the shutter release, then repeated his question. "Why the sigh?"

"Because," she admitted quietly, "I was thinking how nice it would be to hang around here for a while."

Chris hardly dared breathe lest she decide she didn't mean what she'd said. Was she beginning to trust him? The report on her license plates had come early this morning. The plates were stolen. He still wasn't ready to believe she was on the run from the law, but she was running from something, or someone, and had taken pains to keep from being found.

"You could stay, you know?" He handed her the camera.

"I can't. My work..." C.J. gave him the only excuse she could, even while her heart desperately urged her to tell him everything. She was beginning to feel as if everything was closing in on her.

"Do you ever go back and revisit places you've been?" Chris asked when it was clear she didn't mean to elaborate.

"Not so far."

"Think you might make an exception this time?"

"I seem to have a rather short attention span when it comes to places and people," she said with what sounded to him like a touch of wistfulness in her voice.

"Except for your sister."

C.J.'s smile was slow and wry. "Yes, Annie. I hope she's enjoying herself."

"I'm sure she's fine. Are you sorry she didn't come?"

She gazed at him for a long moment, her blue-gray eyes clouded. He wished she would confide in him, tell him what was so obviously worrying her, but she would share her secrets only when she was ready. And he was running out of time. He waited tensely for her answer.

"No," she offered with a sincerity that made his spirits soar. "I'm glad we have this time together."

He let out the breath he'd been holding, then stood and held out his hand to help her to her feet. He didn't release her once she was standing. Her hand felt too good in his, small, warm, soft. As if it had been made to fit.

He wanted her, more than he could ever remember wanting a woman. He wanted, needed, a chance to explore that attraction. Like her, he'd been alone, a loner, for all his life. For too long. He had friends, a few close ones, but no one with whom he felt so emotionally linked. C.J. was a kindred spirit, someone who lived looking over her shoulder, expecting the worst, always searching for the strings attached to whatever she was offered. Restless, seeking a place to belong. Like he'd been for so many years.

Hand in hand, they led the horses up a path to a clearing on the other side of a patch of trees. Chris unsaddled the animals and watered them in the nearby stream, then spread out a sleeping bag on the ground and laid out their lunch, while C.J. finished the roll of film he'd started. This time, though, he was her subject. He obeyed her commands to look up, smile, turn to the left, to the right, hold that pose, look serious, menacing, ornery, sexy.

The last order made him ache to lay her on the sleeping bag and make love to her. Only the uncertainty of how she would view the overture kept him from acting on his impulse.

"You know," he said as she snapped another shot, "I've come to realize you use that camera as a shield."

"Against what?" She gave a short laugh.

"Other people. You can see into the souls of your subjects, without having to reveal anything of yourself."

"That's..." She sat back on her heels, staring at him indignantly.

"Very profound," he supplied with a grin when her protest died.

After a moment, she laughed. "Profound? The indomitable male ego strikes again. Hasn't yours ever gotten you into more trouble than you could handle?"

"Mighty close several times," he said solemnly.

C.J. studied him thoughtfully. She was in over her head, dealing with Matlock and Jordainne, and if there was trouble in Seattle, she needed Chris's help. But it was so easy to misread a person. A mistake now would be costly and the price would be paid not in ridicule endured or cash lost, but in lives. She needed to know more about this man. A matter of curiosity and necessity.

"What happened to your parents?" she asked.

"I was told my mother was an alcoholic hooker."

For several long seconds, C.J. stared at him through the Nikon's viewfinder. His eyes weren't sad or troubled—the eyes of a man who had long ago come to terms with his own identity. Not an easy struggle, she thought, recalling the bits and pieces he'd shared over the past two days.

She snapped the shot, then set the camera on the edge of the blanket. "Did you know her?" she asked quietly.

Chris heard the cautious caring in her voice, something she gave as sparingly as her trust, he felt certain. He would rather she answer his questions about her, but perhaps the best way to get her to open up was to be open with her.

"I was three when social services took me away."

The words came slowly, but with less pain than shone in his listener's eyes. C.J., he saw, felt the fear, the anguish of the small child who was torn from the only life he'd known and thrown into an unfamiliar new world. She hurt for the little boy who had at first withdrawn, then had become hostile and finally a juvenile delinquent.

He moved closer to her as he detailed a couple of terms in detention centers. When he talked of the need to protect himself against other kids, she winced as if she'd received the blows he told about. Chris pulled her against him so her head rested in the crook of his arm. He was seeing a part of her she kept well hidden, he realized. Compassion and empathy replaced the detachment, the reserve she'd exhibited from the moment they'd met.

"I made it tough on myself most of the time," he said with a wry smile. "When you're always spoiling for a fight, you can usually find one."

"Comes from getting a rotten deal too often."

Chris released her and reached for the thermos of warm tea. He filled two cups, handing her one as he sipped from the other. "The way you talk about your family, I have to wonder how you came to be such a cynic. Annie isn't."

"Annie's like Dad. His head was always in the clouds. Mom used to say he was the original absent-minded professor—high IQ, but little common sense."

He set his cup aside and unwrapped the sandwiches, pleasantly surprised she hadn't dodged his query this time. They were making progress, he hoped. He had to know more about her, had to find some way around the emotional barriers she erected, had to find some hold that would bring her back to him once she'd gone to Montana.

In the meantime, she was on the run. Nothing else could explain the stolen tags and why the car she'd been driving was registered to an Arnold Parker of Rome, New York. The man wasn't related to her. Annie had said there was just her and C.J. Oliver was running Parker's name through the computer, checking for outstanding warrants or anything else on him. Was this man a threat, or merely a nuisance to C.J.?

As a little added insurance, Chris had contacted an old friend from his FBI days and asked Nick to do what checking he could on Parker, and on C.J. and Annie. Before Nick got back to him, he hoped to have some answers from C.J. herself.

"You got along with your dad all right, didn't you?" he asked, picking up the conversation's thread.

"No one could fight with him. He was very easy-going. Unfortunately he was also an easy mark. Unscrupulous shop owners, traveling salesmen, anyone who wanted a handout—Dad attracted them like a magnet. In a small midwest town, there's no keeping something like that secret. You can't begin to imagine how awful it was sometimes, knowing people were laughing at him behind his back." She eyed Chris intently. "But then maybe you can imagine how it was."

He nodded. "Humiliation, resentment, outrage, pity. I ran the gamut of feelings regarding my mother, until I accepted that she couldn't have helped herself."

"That pretty much covers mine. I had my escape from rural life all planned out for the day after high school graduation. But Mom died about six months before that..."

"An accident?"

She shook her head. "She'd had heart problems all her life."

"And when she was gone, you couldn't leave your dad and sister to fend for themselves."

"Yeah. Dad died during Annie's junior year in high school. We stayed in Mason Falls until she graduated, then when she was in college, I went out on my own."

"Do you prefer it that way?"

She shrugged. "It seems it's been that way forever." She bit into her sandwich, chewed slowly, then gazed up at him. "What was it like being in the Marines?"

"Rough at first. There were a few guys who liked to start trouble and they found out just which buttons to push to get me fighting mad."

"Was it hard for you otherwise?" she asked with more of the compassion he'd heard earlier.

"It took a while before I began to appreciate the rules and regulations. And the discipline." His sandwich gone, he stretched out on the sleeping bag, leaning on one elbow. "Aloysius, the drill instructor, was one rough bastard, but before I finished basics, he made me see the error of my ways."

"You mean, he taught you it was better to be on the giving end of justice instead of the receiving end?"

"Essentially. He also taught me the art of persuasion, and that a sense of humor could get a person further than a bad temper. And how to handle smart-aleck photographers."

Seeing she'd finished her sandwich, Chris reached over and pulled her down beside him. Her eyes sparkled with laughter.

"What else did he teach you?" she asked.

"That it was far better to be respected and trusted than feared. I spent a lot of time searching for that once I got out. I thought police work was the answer. . . ."

"But people don't trust cops like they used to," she supplied with an emphasis that puzzled him. "How'd you end up here in Wyoming?"

"I came up here on a camping trip. I was tired of the mistrust, the endless violence. . . ."

"Job burnout."

He nodded. "Then while I was up here, there was a forest fire not far from where I was staying. I lent a hand rescuing stranded campers, and after that the sheriff asked for help with keeping thrill seekers and unsuspecting tourists out of the area.''

"And that's how you found your calling."

"You got it. The sheriff needed help on a permanent basis, so I signed on. By the time he retired, I knew this was where I wanted to be." He reached for a small bag nearby on the blanket and pulled out two candy bars.

C.J. chuckled as she unwrapped one. "The big bad sheriff has a sweet tooth."

"It's sort of legendary in these parts. Mr. Parker at the drugstore has a standing order with his suppliers. Wanna take a walk?''

She considered the suggestion, then shook her head. "Maybe later."

"Good," he said, gazing down at her. "I'm too comfortable to move."

So was she, C.J. mused. Had she ever felt this completely at peace? Mind, body and soul at rest. Time to really taste the chocolate, smell the fall-scented air, watch the clouds blow across the sky, feel the warmth of the sun and the coolness of the breeze, to gaze into his rain-forest eyes.

Very slowly he reached out to brush back a stray curl the breeze had blown across her cheek. His hand lingered. With infinite tenderness, he traced the outline of her lips with his thumb.

"You're the most fascinating woman I've ever met," he said softly. "And the sexiest."

C.J.'s breath caught. His eyes were darkened with desire, passion. His work-roughened fingertips skimmed over her jaw and down the column of her throat. He teased her senses with his light touch, tempted her to sample all of this sweet seduction. Her eyes slid closed as his mouth covered hers.

She sighed. This felt so right, so unbelievably perfect. The hint of his beard brushed over her cheek. She moaned softly, restless for more, for all the fire his kiss promised. He wrapped his arms around her, gathering her close until her body was pressed against the length of him. The heat of him burned through her clothes.

Chris tangled one hand in the silky thickness of her hair. The other he ran across her shoulder, down her back, over her hips, molding her soft curves to his hard body. He pulled his mouth from hers to rain a trail of kisses over her jaw and along her throat. Her skin was satin treasure, soft, silky smooth.

The sexual excitement was stronger than ever. C.J. wanted to make love with him. Trying to stop a car with no brakes had made her realize how uncertain the future was, and that made these few stolen moments with him all the more precious.

She'd never felt this close to another person. It didn't matter that they'd only known each other four short days. The bond between them had been forged over their first dinner together. This would be another link, another step to bring them closer still, an intimacy she craved for however long it would last.

For now she would break all her hard-learned rules and live for the moment, experience it to the fullest, not sorting out the meanings or thinking about the consequences.

There was magic in his eyes as he looked down at her, a promise of all the tenderness and passion she hadn't dared to dream existed. He lowered his mouth to hers again. Sparks ignited and burned like wildfire through her veins.

The immediacy of her need for him should have startled her, she thought dimly. Her uninhibited response was so out of character, but then Chris called to that part of her that yearned to play, that begged to be nurtured and healed. All she sought, all she needed, was in his kiss, in his embrace.

She held him tightly, opening her mouth to his exploration, welcoming the powerful assault on her senses. Her fingers wound through the soft thickness of his hair, luxuriating in the texture. She arched against him, her anxious body conveying the strength of the longing that raced through her. He trailed more kisses along the line of her jaw, down the column of her neck. He nuzzled under the collar of her shirt and kissed the sensitive skin there.

"Janey, I want you so much," he said, raising his head to speak against her ear. His warm breath whispered against her skin.

Tiny shivers of anticipation coursed through her. She had no will to refuse him anything he asked for. Desire made her reckless. The need to be cherished by him overwhelmed her.

"I want you, too," she said, her voice breathless.

The simple statement uttered aloud echoed through her being. Her fate was sealed. There was no thought of turning back. There never had been, she acknowledged as he tugged the shirttail free of her jeans.

His eyes never leaving hers, he undid the buttons, one by one. She knew he could read the emotions that played across her features—anticipation, wonder, desire. He slid his palm inside, warming her with the heat of his hand and his gaze. Need coiled deep inside her,

burning for satisfaction, aching, demanding fulfillment.

"You're as beautiful as I'd imagined." He smiled
softly. "And believe me, I've been imagining. How
you would look. How you would feel . . . taste."

Her breath caught as he lowered his mouth to kiss
her stomach, her ribs, the flesh above her lacy bra.
The hint of his beard brought her nerve endings to life,
each screaming out for his worship. His touch was
pleasure and pain, the most exquisite sensations she'd
ever felt. She drank in each one, enthralled, mesmerized by the overpowering feelings.

His mouth brushed across her breasts. Through the
thin strip of lace still covering them, he teased her taut
nipples. Waves of breath-stealing delight rolled over
her. When he unfastened the bra, the tide of emotion
swept her away. He caressed her with tender strokes,
kissed her with hot passion, whispered to her with an
urgency that matched her own.

Ecstasy. His hands treasured, cherished her skin
until she wanted to cry out at the exquisite pleasures
they gave her. Agony. His touch was driving her mad
with longing so strong it was almost unbearable.

He tugged at the zipper of her jeans, impatiently
parting it and sliding his hand inside. His fingers were
hot against her heated skin. Her heartbeat faltered as
he looked into her eyes. The depths of his passion
burned brightly in his gaze, calling to her, beckoning
her closer to the flame.

"I don't want to rush you," he said, his voice gruff
with need.

She pressed her hand to his cheek, smiling shyly.
"I'm keeping up with you," she told him.

He quietly urged her to raise her hips. He laid his palms flat on her skin, caressing every inch of her as he pushed the denim down her thighs, past her knees, off her ankles.

His eyes glowed with desire as he took in the sight of her. "Are you sure about this, Janey?" he asked, his voice husky.

"Yes," she answered, realizing her needs were important to him. She'd been waiting so long for him. All her life, it seemed. She reached for his shirt buttons.

Her fingers shook as she worked the buttons, then pushed the flannel aside. For a long moment she simply stared in awe at the sight of his perfect chest. The muscles proclaimed strength and virility. The covering of curly black hair beckoned her touch. The feel of him was glorious and wonderful. She wanted more, wanted all of him. She pulled at his belt buckle, muttering a soft curse at its stubbornness.

He undid it for her, then hastily dispensed with the rest of his clothing and pulled one end of the sleeping bag over them. Sheltered from the cooling breeze, he kissed her hungrily. Her hands explored the contours of his body, tentatively at first, then more boldly. She trailed her fingertips across his muscled back, down his sides and finally over his firm buttocks.

Chris groaned, his endurance taxed to the limit. He'd never wanted so intensely, never known such fierce need to possess, never felt so acutely alive. He moved over her, burying himself in her heat. She was soft curves and liquid fire. He was the moth driven to lose himself in her flame.

He would never get enough of her sweetness, even if he made love to her every night, every morning. And he wanted to make love to her that often. He gloried in her soft cries of ecstasy. She met his passion without reserve, giving herself completely, entrusting herself to his care. With whispered words and tender caresses, he told her how he treasured the gift she gave.

He rode the tempest with her, holding himself in check until he felt her reach the peak. She tightened around him, her breathing ragged, her voice hoarse, her body taut. He clung to her as together they catapulted off the cliff he'd brought them to, free-falling through space and time, landing in each other's arms.

The wind sighed softly through the fir trees, carrying the secret of their lovemaking up the hillside. C.J. burrowed her face into his sweat-dampened chest, wanting to prolong the intimacy. Forever would not be long enough to spend with him. But she didn't have forever. Only this moment. She laid her palm against his face.

"That was truly incredible," he said. "You were incredible."

"We were incredible."

"The dynamic duo." He nuzzled her cheek, nibbled on her earlobe.

She toyed with the strands of his hair. What they'd just shared she would never know with anyone else. Their bodies had been in unimaginable harmony. Their needs had been fueled by the pleasure they gave each other.

She breathed deeply, aware her senses were amazingly acute. The scent of him tickled her nostrils. His breath skimmed gently over her skin. She wanted to remain there, wrapped for eternity in his strength and tenderness.

C.J. felt the longing stir within her again. She gasped softly when she felt his need for her growing.

He chuckled. "Think you can handle an encore?"

"Oh, yes."

He kissed her, fervently, lovingly, bemused by his readiness to make love with her so soon. The urgency was stronger than ever. She'd given herself to him and he wasn't ready to let her go. He might never be ready. These feelings she stirred, the power and completeness of their joining, were too rare, too wonderful to walk away from. He had to make her see that, and loving her again and again was the only way he could think of.

He raised his head to gaze into her passion-darkened eyes, then heard a rumble in the distance. He looked up at the sky and swore.

"Get dressed," he commanded, scrambling for their clothing. "Fast."

"What's wrong?"

She was already obeying his order as she asked the question. Chris heard the tremor of fear in her voice. Later he would ask her about that, but right now he had other priorities.

"Storm. Coming in fast." He pointed to the black clouds furiously rolling in. Thunder echoed in the air. C.J. didn't waste any time helping him get their gear together and into the saddlebags.

"What are we going to do?" she asked when they'd mounted the horses.

"Outrun a thunderstorm."

"You really think that call to Taylor was from your pigeons?" Jennings asked as they waited for the approaching small aircraft to land on the narrow dirt strip.

"They're your pigeons, too," Matlock reminded the balding man angrily. "Those papers the blonde swiped from Jordainne's desk could put us all away for a long time."

"Diaries, ledgers, journals. Geez, the man's smart enough to make senator, for crissakes. Why the hell was he keeping records like that?"

For the same reason most of us do, Matlock thought, rubbing the salt-and-pepper stubble covering his thick jaw. To protect ourselves from our own people. Jordainne's major screwup wasn't keeping records. It was letting sex short-circuit his brain.

The virile and handsome senator had given Annie Dillon a key to his apartment and told her to wait for him there. He hadn't known she'd somehow gotten the combination to his safe—from his desk drawer, probably, though Jordainne wouldn't admit it. She'd arrived early for the rendezvous, had taken the papers and left before the senator arrived.

From the tiny weather-beaten shack, Matlock watched the twin-engine plane touch down. In the gathering darkness of the storm clouds that rolled over the Montana mountain ridge, the aircraft nosed its way toward the two crop dusters and came to a full stop at the end of the makeshift runway.

Two men got out. The taller one stayed to secure the plane. The other, his brown head bent against the gusty winds, limp-sprinted toward the shack. Anyone else would have appeared ungainly, but he looked rugged and virile despite his impairment. He opened the shack door and shouldered it closed. Steely gray eyes narrowed, hands balled into fists, he glared at the man who had summoned him.

"I'll have the car brought around." Jennings made a hasty departure as the senator's furious gaze flicked over him.

"You were supposed to take care of this without me," Jordainne snarled once he and Matlock were alone.

Matlock worked to hold on to his ever-shortening temper. "You're responsible for this mess. This time you'll be in on the cleanup. Maybe you won't be in such a hurry to make another mistake."

Jordainne growled, but said nothing.

The Dillon sisters would soon be history, at the senator's manicured hands, Matlock thought. He would see to that, and in the process teach the man a well-needed lesson about controlling his overactive libido.

Jordainne should suffer the same fate as Annie and C. J. Dillon, Matlock felt. In the course of his political career, he'd caused more problems than he was worth. Unfortunately Matlock had orders to keep the senator safe. The network was grooming him for bigger and better things. They were damn close to succeeding, but then Annie Dillon's theft of Jordainne's personal papers put those carefully laid plans in jeopardy.

A minor problem, Matlock had assured the men in power, but it had been more difficult to correct than he'd anticipated. The men pressing him for a solution were getting decidedly nervous. They were the type of men it wasn't healthy to disappoint.

He glanced out the window and swore under his breath. The storm was moving in with amazing speed.

Judging from the darkness of the clouds, any minute the area would be deluged with rain. It would be hard enough to pick up the Dillon sisters' trail in this god-forsaken part of the country without the rain complicating the search.

"Let's go." He opened the door, bracing it with his thick shoulder to keep the wind from slamming it into the wall.

"My being here is stupid," Jordainne shouted over the rumble of thunder as they headed for the dark nondescript rental car. "If I'm recognized, this all might just blow up in your face."

"Your face, too," Matlock corrected tightly, opening the rear door for Jordainne, then sliding in beside him. "And I've thought of that. You're going to stay out of sight until we've got our hands on those two."

"Then what?"

Matlock smiled grimly. The golden boy, Alex Jordainne, would be with him all the way on this one. Whether he wanted to or not. "Then you're going to pull the trigger."

Chapter 6

The wind whipped her hair across her face and tore the breath from her lungs. C.J. clutched the reins with every ounce of her strength.

"The Hawkses' farm is the other way," she shouted to Chris over the pounding of hooves and the thunder chasing them.

"Too far."

As if to corroborate that, lightning arrowed across the sky, thunder on its heels. Then came the rain. Cold, fat drops plopped heavily on her head and back, slowly at first, then in a pelting downpour. There was no time for questions about their destination. All their concentration was devoted to getting the animals, and themselves, safely to shelter.

They crested a ridge. The shadow of a huge house loomed in the distance. She followed Chris through the trees, down a gently sloping hill to where the ground leveled off. Without pausing, he raced for the rear of the house. C.J. kept pace with him. Heads bent low over the animals' necks, they rode under a high redwood deck.

Laughing, she swung from the saddle and into his waiting arms. She clung to him, feeling wildly alive and free.

Gone was any trace of fear in her expression. Her dimple had deepened with merriment. Her eyes danced with life. Her delicate face was flushed with exhilaration as it had been during their lovemaking. Chris buried his nose in her hair, breathing in the smell of rain and apple-scented shampoo. He pressed her close to him, molding her entrancing curves to his hard planes. He drank in the joyful abandon in her ringing laughter and knew that everything he'd ever longed for was in his arms.

And he knew he wouldn't be able to keep her there for long.

"You really know how to show a city girl the time of her life," she quipped over the roar of thunder. "Where are we?"

"Home." He pushed the wet hair from her face and grinned down into her puzzled expression.

"You live here?" The place was so big for one person. The deck overhead was half the size of her D.C. apartment.

"Me and Charlemagne."

Something nudged the back of her leg. C.J. looked down at the Doberman whose head nearly reached her waist. She tightened her grip on Chris's arms. When he rubbed the creature behind the ears, she relaxed somewhat. The dog licked his master's hand, then shook himself dry from head to hind end.

"Charlemagne," Chris growled. "If we weren't already soaked, you beast, I'd leave you out here."

Unconcerned with the reprimand, the dog sauntered over to the door and disappeared through the hinged cutout at the bottom. Chris reached into the saddlebags, pulled out C.J.'s camera bag and equipment and passed the things to her.

"Go on in through the basement," he told her. "Up the stairs into the kitchen. There are towels in the drawer beside the oven if you need to dry any of your things."

"What about you?" She flinched as lightning struck nearby. The horses whinnied and stamped nervously.

"I'm going to see to the animals first. It won't take me long. Go on before you catch cold."

The rain cascaded off the deck above in waves. The wind roared with abandon. Thunder boomed in explosion after glorious explosion. Lightning seared the air, hot and uncontrolled.

It was the way their passion had been, wild and uncontained. What had come over her on that hillside?

Startled as much by her thoughts as by the storm, C.J. followed Chris's directives. The door was unlocked. She dashed inside and paused while her eyes adjusted to the darkness. The basement and garage, she noted, getting an impression of orderly shelves, neatly hung tools and an uncluttered worktable. Charlemagne stood on the bottom wooden step as if ready to usher her upstairs.

"Okay, fella," she said, approaching cautiously. "Lead the way."

The door at the top of the stairs was open. She located the light switch on the right, then set her camera equipment on the butcher-block island and glanced around. From the self-cleaning oven and double-wide refrigerator to the microwave, the kitchen was surprisingly up-to-date. And spacious. A room for working side by side with someone, she mused, draping her soggy jacket over a chair, then examining the wide-angle zoom lens and filters for water damage.

"I should have paid attention to the weather, knowing how fast it can turn bad," Chris said, shedding his wet jacket as he walked in a few moments later. "If anything was ruined—"

"Everything seems to be in good shape."

"I'll say," he murmured appreciatively.

His gaze strayed to her shirtfront. C.J. knew without looking that the wet material molded provocatively to her breasts. Her nipples hardened as she recalled the feel of his hands on her skin. She cleared her dry throat.

Now was a fine time to wonder about the wisdom of making love with the sheriff, she admonished herself. She shouldn't have done it the first time, but wise or not, she wanted to do it again, and again. And she would keep on wanting this man long after she was gone from this place.

How could her emotions have become so hopelessly tangled in so short a time? If she survived this mess Annie had handed her and lived to be one hundred, C.J. knew she would never find anyone like Chris, anyone who could make her ache with such single-minded intensity. How could she leave him? But how could she stay? Even without the danger following her, she would soon feel the urge to move on.

"What about Annie?" she asked to take her mind off her disturbing thoughts. "She'll be worried about us."

In answer he picked up the telephone and dialed. "It's Chris," he told the person on the other end of the line. "We made it back to my place, but we're soaked." He listened for a moment, then said, "That would be great." He hung up. "Sara's going to drive Annie over in my Jeep once the rain lets up and her son collects the kids. Bill will bring the trailer for the horses."

"That's a lot of trouble for them to go to."

Chris shrugged. "Around here we don't think of it that way. We just do what we can to help each other out."

Would that apply to her situation? C.J. wondered, fingering the camera bag's strap. In her experience, a friendly hand was always a fickle hand, and help was offered only when there was something to be gained. Could a thousand miles and a few state lines actually make such a big difference in human nature?

"All that taken care of?" Chris inclined his head toward the equipment spread over the island top.

She nodded.

"Then let's find some dry clothes."

He took her hand and led her through the kitchen, past the great room and up a set of carpeted stairs to his bedroom. The king-size bed sat in the center of the far wall between two picture-paned windows. Directly above was a skylight nearly as large as the bed itself.

Seeing the heat in his eyes, C.J. realized he wanted to pick up where the storm had interrupted them. She was more unsure than before. His house was clearly built with a future family in mind. She had no business being here.

But wise or not, she wanted another chance to experience the unfathomable depths of their passion. She might never see him again. Her car would be fixed tomorrow or the day after, then she would be back on the road. Just her and Annie against professional killers. That thought made her shiver.

"We'd better get out of these wet things." Chris went into the bathroom off the walk-in dressing area and returned with two thick towels.

He blotted the ends of her hair. C.J.'s breath caught as his eyes caressed her face, traveled across her shoulders, then settled on the buttons of her shirt. He unfastened the top one, then paused.

"Would you rather I didn't?" he asked, his voice hoarse with need.

She shook her head, knowing where things were headed, yet powerless to stop them. The lure of loving him, of being loved by him once more, was too strong. She didn't protest as he slipped the shirt off her shoulders and gently brushed the towel over her damp skin. With excruciating slowness, he worked the front hook of her bra. The lace whispered to the floor at her feet. He cupped her breasts in his warm palms and sighed.

A sound of contentment and longing. A sound that awakened her own needs and sparked fantasies to life. A sound that begged her to give all of herself to him and promised it would be returned twofold.

She unbuttoned his shirt. Stepping close to wrap her arms around his waist, she buried her nose in his chest and inhaled the rain-fresh smell mixed with the scent of him. He shrugged off the damp flannel, then bent to catch the corner of the bedspread and blankets.

Keeping one arm around her, he yanked the covers aside. He eased her jeans down her narrow hips, gently lowered her to sit on the edge of the bed, then knelt to pull off her wet running shoes and socks. He tugged her jeans off her slender legs, letting his hands and gaze linger admiringly for a moment before he urged her to slide under the blankets. When he'd dispensed with the remainder of his own clothing, he lay down beside her.

She welcomed him with a kiss that made his heart pound as hard as if he'd just finished his morning run. Her arms wound around his neck, clinging to him as she had done on the hillside. Her long fingers ran through his damp hair, slowly, as if memorizing the feel of the strands. Her body pressed against his, giving off a heat that made him burn for more.

He wanted to sample all of her sweetness again, but this time he was determined to spend a long time satisfying his needs. C.J., though, was more anxious. Her hands roamed restlessly over his chest, his back, his hips, silently coaxing him closer. Driving him a little bit insane.

"Think you can handle a little torture?" he asked, laughing when her eyes widened in shock. "Nothing kinky," he assured her. "We were rushed the first time. I'd like to make this time last. Think you can handle that?"

Her dimple deepened with her seductive smile. "If I get to go first."

"Huh?"

While he was still trying to figure out her meaning, she pushed him onto his back and leaned over him.

Her long hair skimmed across his chest as she rained tiny kisses over his skin. The chestnut tresses tickled and teased while her mouth taunted and tormented. She nuzzled his nipples, then flicked her tongue over each one. Chris gripped her shoulders and moaned. Her bold caresses were driving him very close to the edge.

"I've created a monster," he said at her throaty chuckle.

"Complaining?"

Her hands slid lower, past his waist. Her fingers tangled in the tightly curled hair. Chris couldn't speak, couldn't breathe, couldn't think. Her frank perusal made the blood rush through him, hot and fast. She was testing her power, provoking him, pushing him to the limit and beyond.

But he could tell she was reaching the limits herself. Her breathing grew shallow and ragged. Her eyes glazed over with passion. Though he desperately wanted to take her then and there, he let her continue exploring the bounds of her own endurance. When at last she moaned his name in agony and need, it was his turn to chuckle softly.

He pulled her to him, learning her secrets the way she'd discovered his, with his eyes, hands and mouth. His touch was slow and thorough. His mouth moved over her skin hungrily, tenderly. His eyes blazed with caring passion. C.J. moved beneath him, restless, seeking the satisfaction, the fulfillment his touch promised. She craved him with every part of her mind and body.

Arousing him had been its own aphrodisiac. Now that the tables were turned, all her senses were acutely aware. His work-roughened fingertips glided over her soft skin, continuing to stroke, pleasure, light fires. He kissed, caressed, loved every inch of her until she begged for him to take her.

Holding her tightly, gently, Chris answered her urgent plea. Her softness wrapped him in heat, in heart-stopping rapture. He heard her call his name, heard himself moan deeply. He lost himself in the treasure she gave him. Their bodies in tune, they moved together, giving and taking pleasure, savoring the shared intimacy.

He filled her to the depths of her soul. C.J. called his name time and time again, then the breath was driven from her lungs. Pleasure exploded inside her with near-painful intensity. She lay beneath him, weak and sated, completely at peace, content to lay in his arms.

The room was dark. Rain pattered lightly on the skylight. His still-ragged breathing fanned through her hair. His heart beat a frantic rhythm against her breast. She sighed quietly.

"Mmm," he murmured, echoing her satisfaction. After a long moment, he asked, "Am I heavy?"

"A little, but don't move." He felt too good. So right. She wanted this rare contentment to last. Too soon it would have to end. "Maybe we could set a record for staying in bed."

He nuzzled her ear. "I'm all for it, but sooner or later we'd have to get out."

"Why?" She trailed a lazy finger down the length of his back.

"Because Bill and Sara will be here shortly, along with your little sister."

C.J. groaned. "Couldn't we call them and tell them to keep her?"

Chris laughed. "Sure, but I think Bill wants his horses back. And I have to work in the office tomorrow."

"There's nothing I can do to talk you out of that?"

"Nope," he told her, "but you could sure make me anxious to get back to you."

She smiled that seductive grin of hers and Chris was bewitched all over again, tempted for the first time to say to hell with duty. If only he could hold her here forever.

He kissed her once more, leisurely, tenderly, memorably, he hoped. He didn't want her to forget this day, this love they'd made. If she remembered, maybe there was a chance she wouldn't leave. At the very least, he had to convince her to come back, and soon.

To do that he would have to make her realize all they had going for them. Sex was a start, but unbelievably fantastic as it was, it wouldn't be enough to hold someone who couldn't stay in one place for more than a handful of months. It would take a lot to make her stay. Maybe more than he had to offer.

Maybe he would have to settle for this short time with her. That's the way it had been almost all his life—in each foster home, in each new city, each new job. He'd never been good at "settling." Then he'd come to Wyoming and had found contentment.

Now C.J. had come along and made him realize there was still something missing from his life. With her he'd been given a taste of something he'd never had before. Would he again have to settle for less than he wanted, than he needed? Could he accept that?

Reluctantly he pulled his mouth from hers and turned on the nightstand light. He slid out of the bed and reached for his clothes on the floor, swearing softly because he'd forgotten to dry them. He walked over to a chest in the dressing room, dug in the bottom drawer for a set of sweats and tossed them to her on the bed.

"Those shrunk in the wash," he said, pulling out another pair of sweatpants and stepping into them. "They're still big for you, I'm sure, but it's the best fit I can give you while I send your clothes through the dryer." He tied the drawstring, then smiled at her. "Meet you in the kitchen when you're decent."

"Decent?" She sat up, letting the sheet pool provocatively at her waist. "How's that?"

It—*she*—was magnificent. Chris reached down and caught her bare shoulders. "Lady, do that again and I might be tempted to toss you in jail and throw away the key, just so I can keep you here."

She smiled, but he saw the shadow of panic in her eyes, so he backed off on the teasing. He kissed her lightly, wondering how much longer it would be before she trusted him enough to tell him what it was that made her look so afraid. He would give her a chance to talk over dinner, he decided, ruffling her hair playfully before collecting their wet clothes and leaving her to dress. Surely she would tell him now. After what they'd shared, how could there be any secrets between them?

For several long moments after he'd left the room, C.J. sat alone in his bed, listening to the gentle rain, wishing there was an easy answer to her dilemma. And while she wished for the impossible, she thought wryly, why couldn't the answer be written on the skylight?

Why couldn't she have met Chris before now—six months ago in Boston, a year ago in St. Louis, before that in Miami or New Orleans? Why did it have to be now, when there was so much at stake, and so little time to explore this attraction between them?

His mention of jail had brought back all the fears she'd managed to put aside for the day. Add to those some new concerns. She was becoming more emotionally involved with Chris than she wanted to be. She didn't want to be attached to him. She'd been emotionally tied down to some person or another for as long as she could remember. Annie was responsibility enough. C.J. wasn't ready to take on another, not even Chris.

But the love they'd made... The memories they'd created today would be with her for a very long time. Bittersweet and painful. But that was the future and she still had the present to deal with.

Would what she'd shared with Chris make him more inclined to listen to her side of the incredible mess with Jordainne, if she confided in him? Or would he suspect her of playing on his attraction to her, of using him and his position as sheriff to keep her and her sister out of prison? It wasn't true, but would he believe she'd simply surrendered to her own passions? Or would he realize that with the threat of death, she would stop at nothing to save herself, and Annie? Yes, he would know that much about her.

Feeling very weary, C.J. carried the sweatsuit into the bathroom. She splashed water on her face, rolled up the sleeves and legs of the long sweats as she put them on, then made her way downstairs past the carpeted great room.

The Doberman blocked her path into the kitchen. She moved to the left. The dog moved to the left. She moved to the right. The dog moved with her. It didn't bark or growl. It didn't wag its stub of a tail, either. The creature had been calm enough earlier, but there was no telling what was going through its mind now, and she wasn't taking any chances with that mouth of razor-sharp teeth. Warily C.J. peeked around the animal. Chris wasn't in the kitchen, but she heard him whistling from a room off the entrance from the basement.

"Chris," she called out in a shaky voice.

"In here," he called back. "Putting the clothes in the wash. Our jeans were pretty muddy."

He didn't come out, though, as she'd hoped. She waited to see if the dog would follow the sound of his master's voice. To her dismay, it continued to stare up at her with huge eyes.

"Um, what do I do about the dog?" she finally managed, her voice still uncertain.

Chris peered around the corner of the laundry room, smiling at the sight of the dog standing in front of her, its head cocked at a curious angle.

"Take his picture," he suggested. "He looks as if he's posing for you."

"Very funny. Besides, my camera is over there and I'm over here, and he's in between."

"Then why don't you pet him?" he prompted, crossing his arms in front of his still-shirtless chest that snagged C.J.'s attention. It should be illegal for a man to be so damned sexy it made a woman's mouth water at the sight of him.

"Because I'd like to keep my hand."

His grin widened. "Chicken. Charlie won't bite. Unless you've got a gun."

"The word is cautious, not chicken. Every place I've lived, dogs like this eat people like me for between-meal snacks. And what does a gun have to do with anything?''

''That's the only thing I've found that upsets him. First time I took mine out in front of him, he went crazy, barking, growling, snapping. I figure whoever dumped him in the woods might have shot at him to scare him off.'' He stopped, waiting for her or Charlemagne to make a move. ''Trust me.''

But could she trust the animal? she wondered. ''Pet him?'' she said when Chris continued to watch her.

He nodded. She raised her hand very slowly, extending it for the dog to sniff. To her surprise, the animal licked her enthusiastically. His hind end wagged back and forth eagerly. He nudged her hand. Laughing, she rubbed him behind the ears as Chris had done under the redwood deck. The dog moved aside as she took a step into the kitchen.

''Okay, Sheriff, you win this one.''

''And you've made a friend for life.'' He opened the refrigerator. ''Hungry?''

More for him than for food, she silently acknowledged, studying the planes and muscles of his bare torso. She wanted to touch him again, caress him. It would be a very long time before she forgot him, if ever.

''Janey?'' He frowned over at her.

She blinked, realizing she'd been so preoccupied with already missing him, she hadn't answered him. ''Yeah. I guess I am a little hungry.''

''Good. How are you at grating cheese and chopping onions and green peppers?''

''About as good as I am at photography.''

He tossed her a square of cheddar cheese. She caught it, and the pepper and onion he pitched to her next. As she grated and chopped and he heated the chili he'd put together the night before, they chatted. She must have made the appropriate responses, but they were automatic, unconscious.

She couldn't stop thinking about him. For once, she had a compelling wish to stay with someone, with him. Fear of what she faced once she left had a lot to do with the unusual feeling, she knew. But working beside Chris, she was aware of how deeply she'd come to care for him. It was so unlike her to become emotionally entangled with someone other than her family. There was no denying her feelings for Chris, though. She could imagine staying there, sharing his house, his kitchen, his bed.

But how long would she be content? And how did he feel about her? He'd shown her unimaginable tenderness and affection in his lovemaking, but she had come to realize he was thoughtful and generous by nature. Was the way he'd made love with her merely an extension of that? Would he want her hanging around until her innate restlessness sent her packing, or was he content that she would soon be leaving?

More questions, and no answers, she thought as they ate in front of the stone fireplace. Should she take her chances and trust him? Warmed by the flames and the heat in his eyes, she examined his strong character-lined profile. He wouldn't easily accept her claims about a crooked FBI agent with an impressive career and the country's favorite son. Duty would require he investigate. His inquiries would bring Matlock down on them, and put him in as much danger as she and Annie were in. Should Matlock succeed in killing them, Chris's life wouldn't be worth a nickel.

She needed help from someone who could offer her and Annie a measure of protection, but the thought of anything happening to Chris because of her was a physical pain, a stab through her heart. The extent of her concern for him stunned her.

He may have been a loner at one time, but that was in the past. Now he was ready to have a family. The house was evidence of that. He would make a wonderful husband and father, she thought, sad at the mental image of him having children with another woman.

"Why aren't you married?" she asked to dispel the illogical jealousy.

"I guess I didn't want to make the same mistake twice."

"You were married before?"

He nodded. "I've never told anyone else in these parts, but when I lived in Phoenix I met Marlene. Looking back on it, I think I was lonely and she wanted to get out from under her parents' thumbs."

"Was she young?"

"Eighteen. I was twenty-five."

"Quite an age difference."

"Too much, really, when the people involved are that young. Marlene was cute and I was available and interested, but that's all we had in common. She wanted someone she could talk to, communicate with. At that time, I wasn't good at things like that."

He was still a private person, but with C.J. he was different. It was easy to share his feelings with her, his dreams, even some of his fears. And his passion. He'd never given himself to another person so totally as he had when they'd made love. But he'd wanted, needed, to give her everything he had.

"All my life before that I'd had to close myself up," he continued quietly. "Other kids, even some of the adults around me, would pick up on weakness or vulnerability and use it against me." He shrugged.

C.J. thought of the boy shunted from home to home, and the young man thrown into a detention center. No one to care for him and no one to care for. But she sensed he was ready to share his life with someone.

Occasionally she'd longed to be on her own, without the responsibility of watching after her father, or Annie. But on the whole she wouldn't have changed her life. She might have felt alone at times, but she'd never lacked for love. Chris deserved to have that happiness and love that came with a family.

"How about you?" he asked. "You play your cards pretty close to your chest."

She gave him a sad smile. "Dad was so gullible. Such an easy mark. Annie, too. Honest, open. People in Mason Falls took advantage of them. Dad never knew a stranger, never mistrusted anyone no matter how often he got fleeced. He couldn't handle finances at all. From the time I could add and subtract, Mom had me helping her balance the checkbook, pay the bills, plan the family budget. All those were foreign concepts to Dad."

"So you grew up early, then when your mom was gone, you stood between him and the big bad world, like you do with Annie."

She nodded. "Guess that's why I've never had a serious relationship."

"What about the guy Annie mentioned at breakfast yesterday?"

"Marty Kendall," she said, glowering. "He drove home all the lessons my mother taught me. All the while he was conning me, he was taking Dad for money. I still can't believe I was so stupid."

"We all make mistakes. You shouldn't be so hard on yourself."

A ghost of a smile lifted one corner of her lovely mouth. "Old habits..." She reached for her beer.

Chris took a long swallow from his own bottle, wondering how best to get to the subject uppermost on his mind. He had to know what kind of trouble she was in, why she was running. He couldn't let her disappear from his life without any trace, couldn't let her leave not knowing whether danger waited for her. There was no good way to pry, so he plunged in.

"What brings two city girls out to the Wyoming wilderness?" he asked. "You never did explain."

His change of direction caught C.J. by surprise. Her breath stuck in her lungs. "Billings," she said in a rush. "That magazine job I mentioned yesterday. This is great chili. A Texas recipe?"

"Nevada." The reserve, the evasiveness, again. Would he ever be able to get around it? Chris wanted to kick something in frustration. "Got it from a guy in Reno. What about Annie?" he asked, refusing to be deterred. "Why did she quit school to follow you across the country?"

C.J. shrugged. "She was ready for a change, too. I enjoyed the riding today. You really know the terrain. You must spend a lot of time outdoors."

"As much as I can." He set his beer on the coffee table and caught her hand in his. Her evasiveness told him plainer than words that the trouble she was in was serious. He was determined to find out what had sent her running. He brushed his thumb over the satiny inside of her wrist.

"I enjoyed being with you today," he said, trying another way around her barriers. He draped his arm over her shoulder and drew her close. "Billings is only three hours or so away from here. I have some vacation time coming. I could go with you, help you find a place and get settled."

She stiffened. "Thanks, but Annie and I are old hands at that. Then I suppose you are, too, seeing you've moved as many times as I have. I keep thinking one day I'll settle down somewhere long enough to actually buy some furniture of my own, or maybe get some of Dad's antique pieces out of storage. Maybe even set up a darkroom, instead of the makeshift ones I've always had to use."

They fell silent for a while, each staring into the flames. C.J. mulled over his offer to go with her to Billings. He felt something for her, she thought with a surge of elation. He wanted to see her again. But the joy was soon replaced with uncertainty. Would he change his mind about wanting to be with her once he knew she was on the run? What would he do when he discovered the trouble she was in?

She would have to take a chance, she decided. She had to trust him. What other option did she have with Keith unable to help her? Better the devil who possessed a large measure of integrity than the devil completely without scruples. She couldn't run blindly to Seattle when she still had the feeling Keith's accident was related to his background check on Hal Jennings.

When she told Chris about her predicament, she would stress the ruthlessness of the men hunting for her and Annie. That way he could take whatever precautions necessary to protect himself as well as them.

"Chris . . . I . . ." She stopped as the phone rang.

He sighed as it rang a second and third time, then reluctantly got up to answer it. "Yeah," he said tersely. When he discovered who the caller was, his tone changed from annoyed to exuberant. "Hey, buddy. About time you got back to me. What have you got?"

Deciding his phone conversation might take a while, C.J. settled back on the cushions he'd tossed on the floor. His voice was as warm as the flames licking the burning logs. She let the sound wash over her, let herself enjoy it and this moment.

Here, with him, she felt a calm she'd never known. No restlessness, no desire to run from him, no burning itch to explore new places and faces. Interesting, this change in her, she mused, draining the last swallow of beer from her own bottle.

"That bad? Are you sure?" Chris asked his friend in an undertone. C.J. didn't hear much more of the conversation until he began to discuss the weather. "Yeah, the rain's been heavy. If it keeps up during the night, it may take most of tomorrow morning for the river to get back to its banks. I'll give you a route around it."

He gave his directions in detail, including various landmarks and a place to stop for gas and coffee. "See you tomorrow then. At my office."

With a soft sigh, he hung up and returned to C.J.'s side, sinking back onto the cushions and pulling her close to him. "A good friend?" she asked, laying her head in the hollow of his shoulder, feeling sheltered, at peace.

"Nick Talbot. He and I go way back." He took a strand of her hair, wrapping the curl around his finger, seeming to study it with an odd soberness. "All the way back to my FBI days."

Contentment vanished. His words hung in the air. Her chest tightened, trapping her breath. "You didn't tell me you were with the FBI?"

"For five years. In Los Angeles to begin with, then after a year I transferred to Sacramento, then to Denver, finally Salt Lake City. That's where I got out."

"And your friend stayed in?"

"He's with the Federal Marshals Service now."

One duty of a federal marshal was to transport prisoners from one facility to another, and Marshal Nick Talbot was coming to Northfield tomorrow. And Chris had said it was about time the man got back to him, so he'd apparently asked his friend to check out something. Or someone. The coincidence stunk. The walls were closing in on her, and she couldn't get away.

"Why is he coming here now?" she asked, feeling beads of sweat dot her forehead. "Business or pleasure?"

"Nick's been swearing he'll take some time off and come up here. He's finally decided to make good on his promise."

Chris didn't like to lie, but he sensed C.J.'s nervousness. It had started when he mentioned his FBI days. He didn't want to spook her into clamming up completely. Nick hadn't given him any information other than the situation was dangerous and that he should be cautious of other strangers that might show up in the area.

Dangerous. The word still echoed in his mind. As did Nick's final warning for Chris to keep tabs on the two women at all times.

Chris hadn't answered her, C.J. noted, not completely. "Your friend's trip here comes sort of out of the blue, doesn't it?"

Chris shrugged. "His work is like that. He doesn't always know when he'll finish a case, or if he'll get handed another." He let go of her hair. "What were you going to tell me before the phone interrupted us?"

"I, uh, I've forgotten."

It was dark. Matlock was tired, cold and soaked by the heavy rain. He was closing in on his quarry. He could feel it. With the knowledge came the adrenaline rush that pumped renewed energy through his veins. C. J. Dillon and her scatterbrained sister would pay for all he'd gone through. After that, he would take a vacation. A permanent one. Someplace sunny and warm.

Jordainne clutched his sleeve. "Are you sure—"

Matlock pulled his arm free. "I know what I'm doing," he growled as the hotel door lock clicked quietly. With the utmost care he opened the door inch by inch until they could walk inside.

Jordainne whispered a curse. "This is insane. What happens if we get caught and someone recognizes me?"

"Then you'll take the consequences like the rest of us," he hissed, as fed up with Jordainne as he was with Jennings. If he had the authority he would dispose of the two whiners, but he didn't and the men at the top had plans for the bastards. He wondered if that would still be the case if the heads of the network had to deal with Jennings and Jordainne every day.

"The senator's right," Jennings whispered. "If we get caught—"

"Then make sure we don't," Matlock ground out in an undertone as he peered around the dark lobby.

They'd pulled into Redman several hours ago to find the place virtually deserted. There'd been lights on in the hotel diner, though, so they'd decided to wait and watch. If the Dillon sisters were still holed up in this forsaken town, Matlock didn't want to chance being spotted by one or both of them. He'd told Jennings to pull into the gas station and park out of sight at the rear of the building.

He could have walked into the diner, flashed his ID and questioned the woman behind the counter about C.J. and Annie Dillon. But the fewer people aware of his presence here, the better.

So, for several hours, they'd watched the hotel from the car. During the whole time the only activity was when the woman with the long black braid turned off the lights, closed up and left. With her head bent against the driving rain as she raced to her own car, she hadn't even noticed the black sedan across the street.

Matlock had waited another thirty minutes, then decided they might as well gas up the car before checking out the hotel. While Jennings filled the sedan's tank, Matlock had nosed around the station's garage. That's when he'd found the red car with the New York license plates.

The car had to belong to the Dillon sisters. But were they still in the town? Or had they found other transportation?

Satisfied they could check the hotel in secrecy, he tiptoed up the stairs. He sent Jennings to check the two rooms on the right and kept Jordainne with him as he turned the knob to the door in front of him. It was locked. In his peripheral vision he noted the doors to the two rooms Jennings checked had been unlocked.

"Our job is almost done," he whispered.

Seeing Jordainne's face in the next flash of lightning, Matlock smiled to himself. The man was about to be ill—from fear and thinking about what he would have to do. He had enough sense to know Matlock was determined the senator's hands would get dirty this time.

He motioned Jordainne to flatten his back against the wall. The intermittent lightning afforded only brief flashes of illumination, but Matlock didn't need light for what he was going to do. With practiced ease, he picked the lock. Pulling his revolver silently out of the shoulder holster, he entered the room.

Chapter 7

C.J. lay in the darkness of Chris's guest room, unable to shake the feeling that the walls were closing in on her. Over and over, the questions and recriminations whirled in her mind. Was he on to her? He'd been very preoccupied after that phone call from his friend. Was he suspicious?

Had she inadvertently led her sister into a trap set by Chris? She'd been very shortsighted where he was concerned, had allowed herself to get lost in the emotions and sensations she had never experienced before him. She should never have gotten so involved with him when all her thoughts and energy should have been focused on her problems, not on making love. She'd allowed herself to relax when she should have been at her most wary.

When the phone had rung, she had been about to confide in Chris, but after learning that Nick Talbot was with the Federal Marshals Service, she knew she had to do some more thinking first. She couldn't take any chances with their lives.

Annie had arrived soon after Talbot's call, and thankfully had put an end to private conversation with Chris. There was no way C.J. could have dealt with her own fear and panic and continued to make small talk with him for the rest of the evening.

Having her sister with her solved one problem, but the heavy rain created another. According to one of Chris's deputies, the two direct roads to Redman were flooded. The only way Chris could get them back to the motel was if he drove miles out of his way, so he'd offered them the use of his guest room and a home-cooked breakfast in the morning. Enthralled with the house, and still intent on playing matchmaker, Annie accepted before C.J. could object.

Then Shari called to tell Chris she'd closed the diner and the hotel because her mother needed help getting her few head of cattle to higher ground. Though it wasn't normal duty for a deputy, Chris dispatched one of his men to help them, and had the office calls forwarded to his house.

That left C.J. and Annie with no choice but to accept his hospitality for the night. Alone with Annie in the guest room, C.J. couldn't concentrate on anything other than the chilling fear coursing through her. The storm outside raged with renewed vigor. All the while, the sense of foreboding needled her. Long past midnight, C.J. lay awake, mentally replaying every moment she'd spent with Chris.

He'd been curious about her from the start, but lately his questions had become more pointed, harder to evade. She should have wondered about that, would have, if she hadn't been wrapped up in her own need to be with him. Why had she let her emotions control her so completely? She'd been inexcusably careless.

Annie rolled over in bed. "Are you going to tell me what's wrong?" she asked groggily. "You've been upset all evening."

"I thought you were sleeping," C.J. said, startled out of her mental self-censure.

"I was, but I woke up and couldn't help but notice you're still up. What's wrong?"

"Wrong?" C.J. echoed. If Annie had sensed C.J. was upset, had Chris also picked up on it? She'd caught him studying her several times during the evening. There had been desire in his gaze, but with the interest was something else she couldn't put a finger on, something that had disturbed her.

Annie yawned. "You've been pacing ever since we got into this room."

"I haven't moved a muscle—"

Annie sighed. "Mentally pacing. My guess is the only reason you aren't actually on your feet is you don't want Chris to know you're awake."

At times like this C.J. hated her sister's rare flashes of perception. "It's nothing. Go back to sleep."

"All right," Annie grumbled, yanking the blankets over her shoulder. "You're always telling me I need to grow up, but you keep treating me like a kid."

"I'm sorry." C.J. understood her sister's hurt at being left out, but the problems that kept C.J. awake were too much for Annie to handle. Her hurt feelings were much easier to deal with than the hysteria that would ensue if she knew half of what was on C.J.'s mind. "It's just that I have a few things to think about."

"Like Chris?" A flash of lightning illuminated Annie's face as she turned to C.J. "Was it good?"

"What?" C.J. asked in a startled whisper.

"Oh, come on, C.J. I'm twenty years old, and although I have yet to indulge in it myself, I do know about sex."

It took C.J. a couple of moments to find her voice. "So what makes you think Chris and I . . ."

"Because he hasn't been able to take his eyes off you for more than three seconds all night. And I saw the way he looked at you when you came in here with me. If I ever did it, it would be with someone like him, only a few years younger." She yawned. "So was it good?"

"Yeah. The best." C.J. was glad the darkness hid her satisfied smile. She couldn't regret one moment of her time with him, though she'd had no right to indulge her own needs when so much was at stake. Her lack of caution, her putting her wariness aside, even for a moment, might well have signed their death warrants.

"C.J.?" Annie asked after a long moment.

"Mmm?"

"Have you given any more thought to telling Chris about . . . you know?"

C.J. sighed. "I almost told him tonight, but he got this phone call from . . . from a friend."

"So why did that stop you?"

C.J. was suddenly very tired of bearing all her burdens alone, but how much could she tell Annie without panicking her? She decided on half the truth. "His friend used to be with the FBI. That's where he and Chris met."

Annie gasped. "Chris was with the FBI? Do you think he . . ."

"Ran our names through his computer, then called his friend to confirm what he found out? I don't know what to think."

From the start, Chris had acted as though his attraction to C.J. was his only reason for sticking close to her. But he might have been keeping tabs on her and Annie so he could turn them over to his friend. C.J. had once thought Chris wouldn't toy with them if he wanted to detain them, but she could have made a mistake reading him. What did she really know about this man? What if his interest was only a front?

"Well," Annie said, fluffing her pillow, "he hasn't arrested us yet, so I think we don't need to worry. Besides, if you made love with him, you must trust him. You'll tell him about everything tomorrow. Good night."

She *had* trusted him, C.J. amended silently. But she'd been wrong before. This time she couldn't afford to make a mistake.

Could someone who had made love to her the way Chris had deceive her? Could passion as consuming as his be faked? Some far corner of her heart refused to believe him capable of such duplicity. His tenderness, his thoughtfulness, his caring. They had to be genuine.

She closed her eyes, summoning up the memories—the feel of his hands on her skin, the taste of his mouth, the fire in his eyes as she'd boldly explored the planes of his hard body. She thought of him alone in his room, of how complete she'd felt in his arms, of how she wished she could stay with him. . . . Though the wish triggered another stab of guilt, she couldn't deny the longing.

When she opened her eyes, traces of sunlight seeped through the miniblinds. She pushed her hair away from her face, surprised to discover she'd slept more soundly than she'd allowed herself to sleep since they'd begun running. Maybe Annie was right. Maybe subconsciously she did trust Chris.

But should she? She was torn between wanting to believe he truly cared for her and knowing she had to face facts, especially his friend's timely arrival and occupation. Coincidence happened, she knew. But since Chris's appearance in her life, they'd occurred with more than usual frequency.

Mike would surely have her car ready sometime today, she thought as she woke Annie and dressed in the clothes Chris had laundered last night. She didn't know where to go for help, but at least if Marshal Talbot had an ulterior motive for showing up in this particular place at this particular time, she would have a means of escape.

Satisfied she was taking every precaution possible under the circumstances, she followed the sound of Chris's whistling to the kitchen. He wore his uniform this morning. C.J. decided she felt more comfortable with him in jeans and flannel. The brown slacks and tan shirt reminded her of his position and power, things she didn't want to think about right now.

She watched him lay strips of lean bacon on a microwave plate, her mind drifting back to memories of the feel of his long, strong fingers as they'd tormented and pleasured her yesterday. Dangerous thoughts given the current situation. She cleared her throat.

His eyes riveted on her with a heat and intensity that made it plain he'd thought about her most of the night. "Morning." He glanced behind her. "Where's Annie?"

"Helping herself to a shower."

Chris reached for a dish towel and wiped his fingers on it as he walked toward C.J. There was an uncertainty in her gaze he didn't like. All night he'd thought of her and the unbelievable love they'd made. With each memory, he'd prayed she would want to stay with him and explore their feelings, and that she would let him help her through whatever trouble she was in. It appeared he still had some convincing to do.

He tugged her into his arms, nestling her softness against him. She stiffened as she glimpsed the determination in his eyes. Before she could pull away Chris settled his mouth firmly over hers. He gave her a taste of his raw hunger, of all the needs he'd held in check as he'd slept alone last night. He held nothing back, knowing he might not get another chance with her.

C.J. was powerless to stop her response to the hot passion. Heat charged through her veins. Desire coursed through her, swift and overwhelming. The current pulled her deeper and deeper into the liquid fire that surrounded her, filled her.

She opened her mouth on a moan of need. His tongue plunged inside, urgent and demanding. She could deny him nothing, she realized with unsettling clarity. She melted against him, entwined her arms around his neck, ran her fingers through the richness of his hair.

It was Chris's turn to moan. He wanted her with a burning intensity. He cupped her bottom in one hand and pressed her into his hardness. She groaned. Chris drank in the sound of her longing. He was lost in this woman, in the heat they generated.

"Excuse me."

Chris blinked his eyes open as the voice intruded. C.J. started. He peered over her shoulder to see Annie standing in the doorway, an impish grin on her pixie face.

"Sorry to interrupt, but I think something's burning. Besides you two, I mean. The oven," she prompted at Chris's blank stare.

He drew in a ragged breath, then reluctantly released C.J. and reached for the oven door. A whiff of smoke rose to meet him as he bent to remove the cookie sheet.

"Ah," Annie said, "my favorite gourmet delight. Blackened sweet rolls."

"Smart alecks run in your family?" Chris grumbled as he dumped the cookie sheet and its contents in the sink.

Her grin widened. "Even C.J. got a share of..." She stopped as Chris's dog sauntered into the room. "Is that a big dog or a small horse?"

Chris chuckled. "Meet Charlemagne."

The creature stared at Annie for a long moment, then ambled over to C.J. When he nudged her hand, she scratched him behind the ears. The dog accepted this, then turned his nose toward the tray of bacon and sniffed.

"Is it my imagination or is he asking for a handout?" C.J. asked.

Chris gave C.J. one of his lopsided smiles, then snapped his fingers. The dog immediately went to stand at his side. "Come on, Charlie. You can have your breakfast in the basement, and when you're finished you can go chase squirrels." He took the dog and the food dish downstairs.

As soon as Chris and the dog were out of sight, Annie leaned toward C.J. "Want me to get lost for a while so you and Chris can..." Her eyebrows rose suggestively.

At the thought of being alone with him, C.J. felt a mixture of panic and pleasure. How she wanted to forget the first and give in to the second. But her responsibilities took priority. "He has to work, and we have other business to take care of."

"Like telling him about Matlock?"

"No. Not yet. I want time to think this through—"

"From every angle," Annie supplied. "Honestly, C.J., you're the only person I know who has to think a problem to death."

"What problem?" Chris asked as he stepped back into the kitchen. He paused, holding his breath, hoping C.J. would finally confide in him.

"The car," she inserted quickly. "I was anxious to find out if it's ready."

And anxious to move on? Chris wondered, scowling at the thought. Why couldn't she trust him? After the way she'd given herself to him yesterday, what made her hold back this morning? She was afraid. He sensed it. Her troubles were pressing on her. He wanted her to turn to him for help and support, but she was in a rush to run from him. And there didn't seem to be a damn thing he could do to change that.

"I called Mike's house before you came downstairs," he told her evenly. "He left the garage early last night because he figured the rain would flood the roads. It'll be later this morning before the water goes down enough that he can get in to finish up your car."

"Then does that mean we still can't get back to the motel?" Annie asked, an oddly thoughtful tone to her voice.

Chris nodded. "I need to take care of a few things at the office. Why don't you and C.J. hang around Northfield for the day? The town's a mixture of quaint and modern, and the people are always ready to pose for pictures."

"Photographs," C.J. corrected automatically as he handed her a loaf of bread and pointed to the toaster. She didn't like this proposed change in her planned agenda. But what could she do about it? Demand he drop everything and take them to Redman so they could sit in an empty hotel while they waited for Mike to show up at the garage? And just what things did he have to take care of at the office?

"Remember that, Chris," Annie said with mock seriousness. "Photographs are not in the same class as pictures."

"So I've been told, but I've yet to see proof."

And so the chatter went, through breakfast, on the ride to Northfield and as she and Annie were introduced to the two men on duty in Chris's office. Then they left to wander the town in the company of one of the deputies, Sam Black.

C.J. felt as if she and Annie were under guard. To keep them from leaving town? She'd tried to refuse the escort, but Chris had been unusually adamant—one more thing that made her extremely nervous about the whole situation.

But she said nothing about her fears as Sam introduced them to one shopkeeper after another. As Chris had promised, people were very receptive to the camera. They were also more than ready to talk about their sheriff.

"No one has a bad word to say about him," Annie commented pointedly over lunch at the drugstore.

Sam positively beamed at the praise of his boss. "People know Chris is no slacker. They can count on him to handle whatever needs handling."

Very admirable qualities. But those same qualities were a definite threat to her and Annie, C.J. thought, staring out the diner window. Across the wide two-lane street was the sheriff's office. There was a four-by-four rental parked in front. Nick Talbot had arrived a short while ago.

C.J. had watched him get out of the vehicle—a tall man with curly dark blond hair and shoulders nearly as wide as Chris's. A man to be reckoned with, his stance proclaimed as he'd glanced up and down the street. The federal marshal had come dressed for a vacation—jeans, chambray shirt, cowboy boots and a down vest. Still, C.J. couldn't shake the distinctly uneasy feeling she had.

Chris hung up the phone and rubbed the bridge of his nose. The tightness there and in his gut had started when Nick arrived. The afternoon was still young and it appeared things were going to get worse instead of better.

"You were right. We've got trouble breathing down our necks," Chris said to his friend.

"Yeah?" Nick's blond brow arched questioningly.

"That was Willie calling from the hotel in Redman. Someone broke into C.J.'s room."

"Interesting coincidence," Nick mused aloud. "First the garage where her car is being repaired, then her room at the hotel."

"Right." Chris drummed his fingers on the desk. "I could accept one break-in, but not two. Not in a place that hardly ever sees a crime of any kind. And not when both break-ins happened during a pouring rain. Whoever did this didn't want to waste time waiting for better weather."

His instincts had failed him this time, Chris thought. He'd felt there was something fishy about the two women traveling through the Wyoming back roads, but he'd convinced himself they couldn't be involved in anything criminal. But they were on the run, all right, though not from an ex-flame. The trouble was much more serious. He'd been had by a pair of bewitching blue-gray eyes, a dimple that occasionally deepened with mischief and a body that curved seductively in all the right places. He'd been blinded by C.J.'s charms, but now the blinders were off.

Thirty minutes ago Mike called to tell him about the break-in at the garage. Someone had gone through C.J.'s car, thoroughly. They'd also gone through the rest of the station and had taken the little bit of cash in the register.

Chris had almost talked himself into believing it might have been done by drifters or teens who'd had too much to drink when Nick walked in and dropped his bomb. Both C.J. and her sister were wanted by the FBI on Unlawful Flight to Avoid Prosecution charges. Once Chris had recovered from the shock, he'd radioed his deputy taking the break-in report at Mike's garage and told Willie to check out Shari's place, too.

He tapped the folder on the desk. "You're sure the APB is for C.J.?" he asked hoping against hope Nick would admit the possibility of error.

His friend nodded. "She fits the description, and she has a sister named Annie who also fits the description. And when you first called me you said you thought she was on the run from something. Has she told you anything?"

"Not about this," Chris ground out bitterly. Was she a criminal? Or someone innocently caught up in an altogether different situation, one he and Nick didn't have a complete picture of?

But if that was the case, why hadn't C.J. trusted him? Especially after all they'd shared. He'd given her everything he had and he'd come away virtually empty-handed. How many times in his life had that happened? He'd needed it to be different with her, but maybe she'd only been using him. He felt his fury rise, as hot and intense as the passion between them had been.

"This agent who put out the APB on them—" he began.

"Frank Matlock."

"You said he's under investigation, too?" Chris knew he was grasping at anything that might prove he'd been right about C.J. No matter how furious he was, he didn't want to believe she'd played up to him only to keep him from arresting her.

"It's all on the quiet, but some people in the bureau think he's dirty. There've been a few suspicious incidents. According to a couple of my friends still with the FBI, they've been tailing Matlock for a few months. They haven't come across anything solid, until now. They tell me he's hooked up with Sen. Alex Jordainne.''

"Jordainne? From Pennsylvania?''

"The one and only. And Hal Jennings, head of the Seattle bureau office... He's been with Matlock for several days, then Jordainne joined them last night at a spot just inside the Montana-Wyoming border. It appears they're all headed toward Redman, Wyoming.''

Chris frowned. What could C.J. be involved in that would include a U.S. senator and two FBI agents? "What the hell is going on?''

"I don't know for sure, but it looks like everyone is after your ladies, including the FBI.'' Nick scratched his head. "Is your deputy still with them?''

"Yeah. I told Sam not to let them out of his sight.''

"I'd bet my gold crowns Matlock and his crew are the ones who trashed the garage and the hotel room, looking for the two women. It won't take him long to figure out there's a sheriff's office just thirty or forty miles away. They'll be here before you know it.''

Nick was right. Matlock didn't know the area. It would make sense for him to enlist the sheriff department's assistance in capturing his two fugitives, rather than chance losing them completely. Chris only hoped his hunches about C.J. were correct and that Matlock was a cop turned bad, after all. But even that didn't explain why she and Annie were running from the FBI man.

Would C.J. talk to him, give him the explanation that would clear her? Or would she still shut him out?

He had to bring his feelings for her under control, had to be able to treat her with the same cool detachment she'd shown him. He couldn't let her do any more damage to his heart.

Fists clenched at his side, Chris walked to the door. "Let's go see what they have to say."

"Maybe if we were to separate them, we'd get better results," Nick suggested.

"You take the blonde," Chris told his friend. "Bring her back here for safekeeping."

That would give him one last moment alone with C.J. He wanted that time, he decided, heading for the drugstore. He had to give her one last chance to trust him.

C.J. felt the warning hairs on the back of her neck prickle. Something was wrong. They should be on their way back to Redman, to see if Mike was finished with the car. Instead they sat in the drugstore diner across from Chris's office, chatting with him and Nick Talbot. Although the other man seemed friendly enough, there was a watchfulness in his gaze, a patient readiness like that of a mountain cat waiting for the right moment to pounce on his prey. He made C.J. nervous.

There was also a distance in Chris's manner that puzzled and hurt her. It was as if he'd said goodbye to her with that brief steamy kiss in his kitchen this morning, as if he'd somehow shut off his feelings for her. The pain that thought caused stabbed through her.

She felt as if the ground had shifted beneath her. While she and Annie had explored the local craft shops that afternoon, C.J. had come to a decision. Time was running out for them. Their car should be ready, but where would they go? Confiding in Chris would be her best bet.

Now she wasn't so sure. She had thought he cared for her, and had been counting on that to turn things in her favor. But the warmth in his eyes was gone. She couldn't read his expression at all. He avoided her gaze whenever possible. She suddenly felt cold inside.

She watched with a sense of apprehension as Nick suggested Annie give him a tour of Northfield's small shopping district and she agreed. Once they'd left, C.J. tried to fathom Chris's mood as he drank his coffee in a heavy silence. He didn't look up at her. His shoulders were squared. Tension radiated from him.

"Quite an influx of tourists around here," he said softly. "You and Annie, and now Nick... Wonder who'll show up next."

He glanced up at her, waiting, expectant, as if he felt she had the answer. As if she would know who might wander this way. This was no casual question. He was fishing, and he already knew some of the answers.

The federal marshal had filled in some of the details she hadn't given. And now Annie was alone with Talbot. C.J.'s alarm escalated to full-scale panic. She had to get to her sister.

Abruptly she stood. "I... I'll go find Annie."

Chris studied her for a moment. He saw the fear in her eyes, and had to harden his heart against the need to plead for her to talk to him. But it wouldn't do any good to beg. She just wouldn't trust him, wouldn't let him close enough to help. He doubted she ever would.

"Sorry, but I can't let you do that," he finally told her.

His words were delivered with cold authority. C.J. froze, afraid to think what that might mean. She

glanced at the drugstore's door, gauging the distance.
It was time to flee. She could feel it in her bones. But
there was nowhere to run and no one to help her. She'd
been counting on Chris to be on her side. Now she
wasn't so sure he would listen to her story. And Annie—C.J. didn't know how she would separate her
sister from Nick Talbot, but she had to find a way.

Clutching her camera bag, she rushed to the door.
Chris was right behind her. His hand descended on her
shoulder. His grip was unshakable. Impersonal. Cold.
Nothing like his warm caresses. She couldn't speak,
couldn't think.

Someone on the street side pushed the door open.
Cold sweat trickled down her spine as she glanced up.
The man's emotionless gray eyes fastened on her. C.J.
tasted terror. She took a step backward, into Chris's
solid chest. His hand tightened on her shoulder.

"Well, Ms. Dillon." Agent Frank Matlock grinned
malevolently. "The chase is over. For good."

C.J.'s heart raced frantically. He looked intently at
the camera bag she held. Her grip tightened on the
wide strap.

He noticed Chris behind her, pulled out his ID and
held it up for Chris to see. "This woman is my prisoner, Sheriff, she and her sister."

C.J.'s heart hammered. The blood roared in her
ears. Her would-be killer stood before her. Behind her
was a stranger, a man she no longer knew. Her breath
caught while she waited for Chris to do or say something, anything. Could she reason, plead, with him?
Would he listen? Was it too late? Those wonderful
green eyes that had once beckoned to her with the heat
of passion now stared at her with cold lethal fury.

"I..." she began, but the words lodged in her throat.

"They're my prisoners." Chris pulled out a pair of handcuffs. C.J. stared up at him, her eyes full of terror. He took the camera bag from her and clamped the cold steel cuffs around her wrists.

It was tearing him up inside to see her so terrified. He wanted to hold her in his arms, to shelter her, to vow he would do everything in his power to protect her. If only she would tell him she'd done nothing wrong, explain why Matlock wanted her. But she remained silent.

She'd left him no other choice. He tugged her arm. "Let's go." His voice was gruff, but he wouldn't apologize for it. As far as he knew she was a wanted woman. That should be the only thing concerning him now, not the fact that she looked terribly vulnerable and frightened, her wrists bound with his handcuffs. He forcefully buried his need to protect her.

"Not so fast, Sheriff. What are the charges?" Matlock asked tightly.

"Grand theft auto to start with," Chris said, knowing that would buy him time to sort this situation out. Though he cursed himself for being a fool, he still couldn't give up the hope that C.J. would confide in him, would trust him just a little. "The reports came in yesterday. The vehicle she was driving is not registered to her, and the plates on it were stolen from a car in New York. I'm detaining her until I can check it out."

C.J. gasped. Chris had known about the car, but he'd never given a single hint of what he knew. Did all that they'd shared mean nothing to him? Fear paralyzed her. Anger stiffened her spine.

"The vehicle was driven across several state lines," Matlock said smugly. "That makes it a federal case. The Dillon sisters are also wanted on other charges that take priority. They're coming with me."

In stunned horror, C.J. saw Matlock extend his hand to grip her arm. What if Chris simply turned her over to him? He'd tried to kill her once already. His determined expression said he wouldn't fail a second time. There was nothing she could do with her hands cuffed in front of her. And Annie. Where was she? What would happen to her?

C.J. turned her frightened eyes to Chris. Was he a savior, or merely a temporary stay of execution? "You can't . . . We have to talk."

Chris silenced her with a stern look. It was too late for talk. She'd used up all her chances. He turned his cool gaze to the other man. "You'll need extradition papers, and proof of your authority to take the women." That would buy him a little more time, but not much. If only C.J. had talked to him sooner . . .

Matlock's jaw knotted. He straightened to his full six feet. "Sheriff, you will hand over Annie and C. J. Dillon to me immediately, or I'll have your badge."

Chris shrugged, though nonchalance was light-years from what he was feeling. The whole setup felt wrong, and he didn't think it was his wish that C.J. be innocent of any criminal charges that made him feel this way. Matlock was entirely too anxious to take custody of the sisters.

"Do what you have to," he told Matlock. "The women stay in my jail until I'm satisfied everything is in order."

Matlock scowled at Chris. "I'll be back with the papers in one hour. She and her sister had better be there when I get back."

His grip tight on her arm, Chris opened the door and ushered C.J. out of the drugstore. As they walked across the street, she saw Matlock walk up to a black sedan and lean down to speak to someone inside. He'd brought reinforcements with him to Wyoming.

Once she was inside the jail, she turned to Chris and held out her wrists, praying like she'd never prayed before that he was on her side. She could feel his fury as he glared down at her.

"You can undo these now," she said with false bravado. "Where did Talbot take Annie?"

"To a holding cell downstairs."

"Holding..."

The coldness in his voice settled over her like a mantle of ice. She wouldn't be able to bluff her way out of this. He was too angry. She stared at the cuffs he made no attempt to remove, knowing now that she should have listened to her instincts, should have told him everything after they'd made love. But after the phone call from Nick Talbot, her innate caution had made her wait. She only hoped she hadn't waited too long, that she hadn't killed all the feelings he had for her.

"You have to hear me out, Chris," she said urgently.

He towered over her, formidable, intimidating, menacing. Any affection or friendliness was gone. The hope that he might listen to her side of things died. He marched her into his office and none too gently dropped the camera bag on his desk.

"What's your game, C.J.?" he countered through clenched teeth. "Cozy up to the sheriff? Let him think you really care, when all the while you're laughing up your sleeve because you've got him hoodwinked?"

"Hoodwinked? Chris that's not—" The biting coldness of the cuffs stung her wrists as he backed her up against the desk and caged her there, one arm on either side of her shoulders.

"Isn't it? Oh, you tried to get rid of me at first, but once you knew I was interested, you couldn't fall in with the program fast enough."

Her chin came up defiantly. "If that's how things looked to you—"

"How the hell else are they supposed to look? You don't seriously mean to tell me you cared? I gave you every opportunity to talk to me, but you never once trusted me."

Chris saw her flinch at the harshness in his voice, but plowed on mercilessly, venting the fury and the frustration he'd kept bottled up for so long.

"You used me," he bit out. "And now you figure you'll sweet-talk your way out of jail. Well, it won't work."

He wanted to shake some sense into her. He wanted to throw her down on the floor and make love to her again and again until they were both too sated to move and she understood just how deeply his feelings for her ran. He wanted to scream out in agony. She was the one woman who could spark his passion like never before. With her he'd shared his most intimate feelings, but that had been a one-way street.

He'd been falling in love with her, Chris realized with another surge of anger, and she hadn't felt anything for him.

"Then if that's the way you feel, I guess we have nothing further to say to each other," C.J. snapped, lashing out in anger.

How could he believe she'd used him? That she'd felt nothing for him? He obviously felt nothing but hatred for her. That hurt. More than she would have thought possible. She felt small, helpless, her hands bound in front of her while she faced down this mountain of a man, but she refused to let him see her pain. Her hands balled into tight fists. The steel cuffs bit into her skin. She welcomed the physical pain. It blocked out the hurt that tore at her heart.

He stared at her for a long moment, his eyes narrowed and his jaw knotted. Then he stepped back, unlocked the cuffs and walked her out of the room.

"Oliver," he called to his deputy, "put her in the cell with her sister." He tossed the cuffs and keys on the nearest desk.

The deputy hesitated until Chris cast a wrathful glower at the man. Oliver eased forward to take C.J.'s elbow.

C.J. refused to beg. Not that it would have made Chris change his mind, anyway. She stared at him with all the coldness she could muster, but inside she was dying.

"What about my camera bag?" she asked.

Chris glared at her for a long moment, angry beyond words. Her camera equipment. She's under arrest and that's all she asks for. He was on the bottom of her priority list and always would be. How could he have let her deceive him so? She could have the damn bag and its contents, for all the good it would do her in a jail cell. But he refused to give in to her any more.

"It stays with me," he said, then went back into his office.

C.J. whirled on one heel and let Oliver escort her through the door and down the stairs. She'd expected darkness and the sour odor of mildew, but she should have known better. Chris would insist the condition of his jail be above reproach. Annie was in the first cell, sitting on the edge of the cot, biting her nails. When she saw C.J., she got slowly to her feet.

"C.J...."

C.J. shook her head, grateful that Annie picked up on her signal and said nothing more until Oliver had locked her in the cell and he and Nick Talbot had left.

As soon as the door upstairs clicked shut, Annie grabbed C.J.'s hands. "You said this is what Chris would do when you told him about us."

C.J. laughed humorlessly. "I didn't tell him."

"Then how..."

"It seems the good sheriff ran the car's license plates through the computer days ago. He's been looking into our background from the start."

"But why did he wait until now to arrest us?"

C.J. chewed her lower lip. She had her suspicions. He'd been waiting for his friend to arrive. But she didn't dare tell Annie that Marshal Talbot had undoubtedly come to take charge of Chris's prisoners and transport them back to Washington, D.C. Didn't dare tell her that Frank Matlock had found them and would be waiting for them outside the jail. Didn't dare tell Annie that her big sister had possibly blown their one chance to get out of this mess alive.

Chris would never forgive her, she knew. But somehow she had to get past his fury and coldness and

make him see he had to listen to her. She had to do
something and there weren't a lot of options.

Annie's grip tightened on C.J.'s arm. "What do we
do?" she half whispered, her eyes full of fear and uncertainty.

"Think," C.J. said, pacing in front of the narrow
cot.

But instead of escape plans, all she could think
about was her fury with Chris. He was being unrea-
sonable—to expect her to have blindly trusted him.
Especially when his position and power spelled potential danger.

Her libido had certainly taken over where he was
concerned, but she couldn't have risked her life, and
her sister's, on a physical attraction.

The man hadn't given her a chance to explain. He'd
decided he had everything figured out and refused to
listen to anything to the contrary. He hadn't even
asked her about Matlock, hadn't said whether he
would turn her over to him, she thought with a jolt of
fear. Damn it! That should be her main concern, but
she couldn't stay focused.

"Damn stubborn cowboy," she muttered, wishing
there was something in the small cell she could kick to
vent some of her anger. Chris had never bothered to
look at this from her point of view. She hardly knew
him. How could he expect her to trust that he would
believe her, that he would take her side over Matlock's? Life just didn't work that way.

He, of all people, should understand. He knew how
difficult relationships could be. Often it was better not
to take the risk of letting someone get close. Chris had
lived most of his life that way, just as C.J. had, and

now he was penalizing her for it. Her hands clenched. She paced faster.

He was about to sign her death warrant, and Annie's. How was she going to get out of this mess? What was he doing about Matlock? Could she convince him to look over the evidence, convince him that Matlock was lethal? Would he realize the kind of precautions he should take?

The matter was out of her hands. She hated that, hated the uncertainty. Even more, she hated having someone else decide her fate. But Chris was calling the shots now and there wasn't a damned thing she could do except wait for his decision. And try to hold the fear at bay.

Still, Chris was an honest man. If she showed him the evidence she had on Matlock, he would protect her. Protect Annie. But C.J. knew that would be as much as he would offer her. The caring, the wonderful tenderness and the powerful passion were gone. She'd killed them. Smothered them with her mistrust.

C.J. dropped onto one end of the cot, drained, empty. She'd lost Chris. She'd hurt him with her lack of trust, destroyed whatever she might have had with him. And now that she couldn't have it, she realized how very much she wanted what they might have shared. She'd fallen in love with him, and that realization settled over her with a heavy despair.

Chapter 8

Chris scowled as his deputy told him C.J. was asking to speak with him. Alone. She hadn't told Oliver why, just that it was urgent.

Chris didn't want to see her again. Not until he could clamp a lid on his feelings for her. That would take much longer than they had. He was afraid a lifetime wouldn't be long enough. But he had to sort through this entire mess and she was the one with the answers.

"Bring her up here," he told Oliver. The deputy nodded once and left.

"Want me to leave you alone with her?" Nick asked.

Chris debated about being alone with her again. So far his judgment hadn't been particularly wise around her. But she had asked to see him privately.

"Give me five minutes," he decided.

That's all the time he would give her. He didn't want to turn her over to Matlock, not until he heard her side of the story. Hell, the man's own colleagues suspected he'd switched loyalties. Chris had to hear what C.J. had to say.

He sat behind the desk and took a deep breath. He needed to prepare himself for the onslaught of emotions that would hit him when he saw her again. To put an end to thoughts of what might have been between them. All the laughter and love they might have shared would never be. He had to forget, to bury the cherished memories and get on with his life.

But when she walked in, he still wasn't ready for the swift jolt of protectiveness that hit him square in his solar plexus. He didn't want to notice how vulnerable and frightened she looked, and how alone. He didn't want to see the haunted expression in her eyes, or to recall how those bewitching eyes had sparked to life when he'd held her in his arms and made love to her.

But the observations and memories were lodged deep in his brain. In his heart.

The need to offer comfort and reassurance raced through him. Before he could halt its course, it reached his heart, and he knew he would carry the scars of his brief relationship with her for a very long time.

"Sit down," he barked to her as Nick walked out and pulled the door shut.

C.J. swallowed uneasily. The coldness emanating from Chris filled the room. She did as he'd commanded, searching his gaze for a trace of some emotion other than anger. She found nothing but the fury she deserved.

"I'm sorry," she said, facing up to her mistakes with him. "I should have realized you were the one person who could be depended on without reservation."

She raised her gaze to his, wishing for a glimmer of forgiveness. It wasn't there. It never would be, she thought grimly. She'd dealt him a mortal blow and she would have to pay the price, knowing each day of her life that she had thrown away the one man who could make her life complete.

Chris watched as she stood and reached for the camera bag on his desk and began pulling out the equipment, setting down each piece with great care. He felt his blood boil and realized that for one extremely stupid moment he'd hoped she would rush into his arms and beg him to forgive her, to still care for her.

"Die-hard photographer to the end," he ground out harshly.

A wounded look flickered in her eyes, but it was quickly squelched. "I deserve that," she said, her voice subdued. "I made a major mistake, not being up-front with you. I lied to you, and I'm very sorry for that. But I never used you—"

"That's what it's called in my book."

C.J. breathed to stall her temper. She hadn't used him. She had cared. He wasn't ready to see that yet—might never see that—but just now they didn't have much time. She ripped the bag's lining, pulled out the documents and laid them on his desk.

"I know you hate me for lying to you," she said, looking up at him. "And I know I have no right to ask you to trust me, but before Matlock gets back..." Her voice faltered at that thought, and at the knowledge that in his anger Chris might want to turn her and Annie over to Matlock just to be rid of her. "Please. Annie and I haven't done anything wrong. These papers will prove it. If you'll, please, just look at them."

Chris studied her through narrowed eyes. He didn't want to give in, didn't want to be swayed by her honest apology, didn't want to have her simple appeal tug at his heartstrings. He wanted to shout that she was only using him again to save her skin, but his heart wouldn't let him. She was in danger and he couldn't let anyone harm her in any way. Still, he refused to wear his feelings on his sleeve.

He reached for the leather-bound diary first. What he read made the knot in his gut tighten. He called out for Nick, pointing to the documents C.J. had laid on his desk as his friend entered.

While Nick peered over his shoulder, Chris studied the papers. With each document he finished, the knot in his gut tightened even more.

"Damn," Nick said in awed amazement. "This is a hell of a lot more than we expected. I can't believe what I'm reading."

Chris, too, could hardly digest the facts before him. How could C.J. have thought she could deal with this on her own? The burden she'd been under. And through it all she'd refused to ask for his help.

"When you called to have me check out your lady," Nick began, "and then I found out Matlock was looking for her, I figured we'd stumbled on to something big. But I never dreamed it would be this big."

"There's plenty of evidence in these pages," Chris said grimly. Enough to make him break out in a cold sweat each time he thought of what would have happened to C.J. had Matlock caught her. The man had nothing to lose and everything to gain if she, her sister and these papers were to conveniently disappear.

"Hell," Nick said, glancing at C.J., "you've given us things we never dreamed existed. And cleared up one major question in the process—the men trailing Matlock said Senator Jordainne hooked up with him in Montana. This explains why. The senator's diary pages, ledger sheets..." Nick picked up another book and thumbed through it. "And his personal address book."

While Nick read over the names in the book, C.J. sat silent, observing the expressions on Chris's face as he examined the other documents. The more he read, the tighter he closed the door against her love. He was going to help her, she knew, but that would be the end of his involvement with her.

She'd given him nothing but trouble and pain in return for the indescribable ecstasy he'd given her. That it was unintentional was beside the point. She would never be able to make it up to him, even if he gave her the chance. And that was not likely.

"Nearly every name in here has a criminal record." Nick frowned down at his friend. "These guys play for keeps."

"For keeps," Chris echoed tightly as Nick picked up the phone to call this new information in to his supervisor.

C.J. was too smart not to realize what she was up against, Chris knew. Hurt by her unwillingness to confide in him, he'd exploded at her, then ordered Oliver to lock her up. Now, as the evidence showed that she was involved in some deadly business, his fury ran even deeper.

Fury at himself for not confronting her earlier. Fury at her stubborn refusal to ask for his help, even in a life-or-death matter. Goes to show how little she cared for him, he thought bitterly.

The woman of his dreams. But she didn't trust him. Had never trusted him, even when their passion had driven them to the edge of madness, carried them to the brink of heaven. She'd been with him all the way. So close. Yet there'd been a chasm wider than all of Wyoming between them. And he hadn't seen it.

"The office is contacting the guys tailing Matlock and sending some people from Cheyenne," Nick said, replacing the receiver on the cradle. "They should be here in a couple of hours."

Then the feds would take C. J. Dillon and her sister back to D.C., Chris knew. Out of his life. He should be relieved, but he only felt empty.

"What do we do with Matlock when he gets here?" Chris remembered the terror in C.J.'s eyes when she'd faced the man.

Nick ran a hand over his prominent jaw. "We've got to get him, and the others, behind bars. How many deputies do you have here?"

"Just Oliver right now. Willie's out on a couple of calls, and Sam and Charlie are off duty. I'll have Oliver get them all back here."

"Good. The more manpower we can get, the better." Nick pointed to the papers on the desk. "I don't know about you, but I'd like to hear the whole story behind these. And how they came to be in that camera bag."

So would he, Chris thought as he walked to the door and opened it. But he wished again that he'd heard it two or three days ago, when he would have had time to set things up to ensure C.J.'s—everyone's—safety. As it was he had forty-five minutes. Or less.

"Oliver," he called out to the tall man at the front desk. "I want Willie, Sam and Charlie back here ASAP. But first, bring Annie Dillon to my office."

"Sure thing, Sheriff."

Chris nodded. Forty-five minutes or less. As he walked back into his office, he wondered if they could formulate any kind of a plan in that short a time.

"Sit down," he commanded Annie when she walked in.

She dropped immediately into a chair. C.J.'s gaze, though, locked with his for a very long moment, her chin at that defiant angle. The woman was stubborn to the core. Chris did not need that. It had taken him most of his thirty-seven years to find the contentment and happiness he had now. He would not allow any woman, no matter how unforgettable, to destroy his peace of mind. He would stop wanting her, needing her, no matter what it took. The alternative would shatter him like a piece of delicate china dropped onto a cement slab.

He willed his own gaze to remain emotionless as she pulled her chair up to the desk and began packing her equipment back into the bag. "Those aren't the only copies I made."

"How did you get hold of these papers?" Nick asked evenly, his face an expressionless mask.

C.J. studied him, then Chris, through narrowed eyes. Hard as she tried, she couldn't read their intentions. "First, I want to know what you're going to do with us."

Chris had to use all his willpower to keep from throttling her. He wanted to lock her up and throw away the key because then he would always know she was safe. The thought almost knocked him out of the chair.

Why the hell had his protective instincts chosen this particular time to go off the deep end, and over a woman who did not want his help? He clamped his hands together tightly. Why couldn't C.J. just accept that he would do all he could to keep her safe? He glanced at Nick, who appeared to be taking C.J.'s wariness in stride.

"I can offer you protection," Nick stated calmly. "For both you and your sister."

"That goes without saying," C.J. informed him, the steel in her eyes adding emphasis. "Annie and I won't be separated."

Chris scowled at her across the desk. "You are not in a position to make demands here."

The harshness in his voice sliced through C.J. She'd been alone for so long, no one to lean on. Other than her family, she'd never had anyone show her the unconditional caring and tenderness Chris had shown her.

With him she'd discovered all she'd been missing. He made her think of possibilities, made her dream, long for what she couldn't have with an intensity that left her feeling hollow.

She'd doomed herself to a life of emptiness without him. Staring at her zoom lens, she took a deep steadying breath to compose herself enough to look up at him.

His forehead was creased. With anger? Or with concern? For her? Was there a possibility that her mistrust had not destroyed everything between them? There was nothing in his face to justify keeping the flame of hope alive, the hope she wanted so desperately. But it would kill her to give it up. She would deal with reality later, if they all made it through this alive.

"I understand my position," she said quietly. "And I know you wouldn't split us up. But . . ." She glanced from Chris to his friend and back to him.

"You can trust Nick."

C.J. nodded, accepting his word of honor. Regardless of how he felt about her, he would do everything in his power to protect her. If she had to put her life in someone else's hands, Chris was a man she could trust. Too bad she'd allowed fear to blind her for so long.

"We're short on time, Ms. Dillon," Nick prompted.

C.J. looked to Annie and nodded.

"I got the papers from Jordainne's safe at his house," Annie said.

Chris bolted forward in his chair, his gaze sweeping from C.J. to Annie. His shock was no less than C.J.'s had been when Annie waltzed in with those papers. She'd been damned lucky to get away with her preposterous stunt.

"How did *you* get into Jordainne's safe?" Chris asked her.

"It wasn't so difficult." Annie beamed with pride at her accomplishment. "See, I worked on his reelection campaign and he was . . . you know, interested in me."

Nick nodded. "The senator has a fondness for young pretty blondes. Everyone in Washington knows it, but he's got enough connections to keep it out of the press."

"I was flattered by his attentions, at first," Annie said. "I thought he was being nice since I was new.

He'd ask me if I liked what I was doing and I'd say it was okay because I was just calling people and stuffing envelopes—''

"Better get to the point," Chris suggested, glancing at the round-faced clock on the wall.

C.J. noted his worried frown and his tense shoulders. Matlock would be here shortly—to collect his prisoners.

"Okay. Sorry." Annie breathed deeply. "After a while he noticed I was good with numbers. He said he admired my talent because he couldn't even memorize the combination to his safe so he'd written it down in the front of his phone book. He put me to work with another woman who collected the contributions. I thought they had an odd system of keeping track of the money. Some checks were listed by the name on the front. They went into one account. Then there were others that went into a special account for a few weeks, then the money was divided up and put into some other accounts."

"Let me guess," Chris said, pointing to a ledger sheet. "This is a list of the 'special' checks."

"And where they came from and where they went. I started keeping records of my own on the sly. See, the senator was getting more and more friendly. Then one night when I was waiting for him because he said he wanted to talk to me, I heard him talking to this one guy. The worm told this guy he owned several companies and that he could launder as much money as the guy could send him."

"Did you get a look at this guy?" Chris asked.

"Yeah. His face had been in the papers the week before because the IRS had charged him with tax evasion. That's when I decided Jordainne was a sleaze and that the weird record keeping was necessary because he was cheating the public like he was cheating on his wife.''

"That still doesn't explain how you got into his safe," Nick pointed out.

Annie paused for another deep breath. "He kept coming on to me, so I decided to play along and collect as much evidence on him as I could. Against C.J.'s better judgment."

"Definitely," C.J. affirmed.

"But he had to be exposed. I went out with him one night and he'd had too much to drink and said something about 'the papers in his safe would keep him safe.' Then a couple of weeks ago, he gave me the keys to his apartment. I went there hours early, found the combination written in the front of his phone book just like he said. I grabbed those papers and carried them out in a shopping bag."

Chris stared, agape. "You just walked in, took the papers, then left?"

She nodded.

C.J. shrugged when he looked at her. "Beginner's luck, I guess. I'd told her to let someone else expose Jordainne, that what she wanted to do was dangerous—"

"That this wasn't a movie script and the good guys didn't always win," Annie finished.

"I thought I'd convinced her, but then she came home with those. We made several copies of everything." C.J. looked at Chris's worry-creased features. His green eyes no longer glowered at her with anger, but they still lacked the warmth she craved. She pulled three keys out of a side pocket in the camera bag and laid them on the desk. "Those belong to safe deposit boxes in Trenton, New Jersey, Kansas City and Scottsdale, Arizona. There's a fourth to a box in Denver. It's on the key ring in the car.''

Chris bounced the keys in his palm, studying them thoughtfully. C.J. longed to throw herself into his arms, to have him hold her, soothe her, love her. But she'd had her chance and lost it. When this was over and he was no longer a part of her life, she would have to deal with the sorrow and emptiness. Her personal prison. A life sentence. If she lived past this day, every day after would be an eternity.

"How did Matlock get involved?" Chris asked her, his expression as cool and detached as his voice.

"We took one copy of the evidence to the FBI office in D.C. He was there. We played right into his hands."

"We trusted that snake," Annie said vehemently. "Or at least, I did. C.J. said we had to be careful."

Nick thumbed through Senator Jordainne's phone book. "Matlock's name isn't in this."

"Or on any of the other papers," C.J. said. "I still haven't figured out how he managed that."

"Fear," Chris offered.

"The senator is sufficiently afraid of Matlock's ruthlessness that he kept the man's name out of everything?" C.J. nodded. "That would explain how Matlock could make Jordainne risk his career by coming here to finish us off."

"Tell me about the car situation," Chris said.

C.J. gave him a succinct explanation on why the car was still registered to the original owner and why she'd stolen the licence plates. Then she sat back and waited.

Chris breathed in relief that she'd given them the facts they needed. But then she must have figured she had little choice, that she either dealt with him and Nick, or she dealt with Matlock. Given the information he'd read through a few minutes ago, she must have decided the sheriff was the lesser threat.

"Why didn't you go to another FBI office? One closer to D.C.?" he asked quietly.

"I wasn't sure how far Matlock's connections stretched," C.J. said slowly. "I have a friend in Seattle, an investigative reporter—"

"Keith Taylor, by chance?" Nick asked.

C.J.'s heart lurched. "How did you know?"

"We had men tailing Matlock. He and Jennings were tailing Taylor. We knew Taylor was checking Jennings out, but we wondered why. And we wondered why Matlock was so interested in Taylor."

"How is Keith?" C.J. asked. "Do you know anything about his accident?"

Annie gasped. "Accident? You didn't tell me—" She shook her head. "That's why you've been so worried."

"I didn't want to upset you...." C.J. frowned as her sister's mouth compressed into a tight line and her shoulders stiffened. Soothing her ruffled feathers would have to wait for now. C.J. turned to Nick. "Then do you know how Keith is?"

"Last I heard he wasn't able to tell anyone what happened, but his condition had been upgraded from critical to serious. He wasn't in any accident, though. Our tail lost Matlock for a while, and the next thing we knew, Taylor was in the hospital. He'd been beat up pretty bad. I don't think it would take a genius to figure out who did it."

"His wife told me he was in a car wreck."

"Matlock was probably standing beside her when you called. Right after leaving her house, he made arrangements to meet Jordainne in Montana." Nick picked up the phone. "I'll have Taylor placed under guard."

C.J. shivered as he gave the orders to the person on the other end of the line. She would have to trust that his associates would keep Keith safe, and pray that her friend would pull through this ordeal. He had to. She couldn't forgive herself if he didn't make it. Granted, Keith had known the risks he was taking, but he'd taken them on her behalf. That was one debt she would never be able to repay.

She slanted a glance at Chris. He studiously avoided her gaze, alternating his attention between the papers on his desk and the clock. C.J. had to accept that he no longer cared for her. The pain tore through her, destroying the last remnants of the hope she'd foolishly clung to. She'd been foolish in everything that concerned him—except for one. Making love with him.

It was the most wonderful thing she'd ever experienced. And the most horrible. He had taught her to hope again. Had taught her to look forward to the future instead of just getting through the day. Had made her see her tomorrows in terms of sharing them with another person. With him. He'd resurrected emotions she had no room for. Now they filled her mind, squeezed her heart.

"So what happens now?" she asked Chris, schooling her voice so it wouldn't betray her heartbreak.

"I'm going to have Oliver put you back in the cell." He held up his hand when she started to protest. "For your safety only."

"I realize that," she said impatiently. "I just don't like being . . ."

"Trapped," Annie supplied. "C.J. always wants to know she has an escape route."

"Thanks," C.J. said dryly, "but I think he's already figured that out."

Chris got to his feet. He needed to find out if the other deputies had made it in yet. Squaring his shoulders resolutely, he marched to the door.

It would all be over soon. C.J. would be gone, taking with her the love, so rare and incredible. The joy that had stolen into his heart little by little until it had filled him to his soul. The anticipation of all the days and nights to come. Jaw clenched against the pain that sliced through his gut, he walked out the door, pulling it closed behind him.

Oliver sat in his chair, his head resting on the desk. The fact that something was wrong had barely registered when Chris felt the cold, hard pressure of a gun at his back.

"All right, Sheriff," Matlock said softly. "Raise your hands nice and easy."

When he complied, Matlock yanked the gun out of the holster at Chris's side. Chris swore silently. He'd been so preoccupied with C.J. and his heartache that he hadn't paid enough attention to details. He should have anticipated Matlock's move.

"You're so anxious to collect your prisoners," he said evenly, "that you're burning your bridges."

"Believe me, Sheriff, I know what I'm doing. When I couldn't track down those two right away, I knew it was only a matter of time before my career was over. Besides," he continued, "I figured if C.J. hadn't already shown you the evidence she has, she'd do it now for sure.''

Because she'd had no choice but to tell him. Chris would not delude himself by thinking otherwise. But even so, he'd let her down. He should have prepared for this eventuality.

''Your deputy was kind enough to open the back door,'' Matlock went on. ''My friend and I wanted to surprise you.''

Chris glanced over at Oliver again. A balding man with a thin nose stood at the counter, near the deputy. There was a gun in his hand. Chris muttered another curse while he worked to figure out a way to alert Nick.

Chris inclined his head toward the man slumped over the desk. ''What have you done to him?''

''He's suffered a rather solid blow to the head,'' Matlock said. ''It was the best method to get him out of the way. A gunshot would have warned you something was going on out here and we didn't want that.''

Chris stiffened at the man's unfeeling words.

''Don't try anything, Sheriff,'' Matlock growled. ''Jennings, cuff the deputy's hands to the chair. Just in case he wakes up before we're done here.'' Once the deputy was taken care of, he gestured toward the office door. Jennings took a position on the right. ''Open it and walk in, slowly,'' Matlock ordered Chris. ''And remember, if anything happens, you get the first bullet. In the back.''

The man would take great pleasure in firing the shot, Chris thought, doing as he was told. C.J. glanced up as he walked in. For a moment her eyes held that haunted look again. Then she spotted Matlock.

Shock and sheer terror flitted across her features. Then a cold resolve settled on her delicate face and slender frame. Chris wanted to go to her, to assure her everything would be all right. But he couldn't lie to her.

He saw Annie clutch C.J.'s arm in what had to be a painful grip. Nick kept his hands on the desk. If he went for his gun, Matlock would shoot. He had nothing to lose.

"You cover the women," Matlock told Jennings. He shoved Chris farther into the room. "Introduce me to your associate, Sheriff, while he carefully puts his weapon on the desk and steps back."

"Nick Talbot," Chris said tightly.

"Federal Marshals Service," Nick volunteered, following orders.

Matlock glanced briefly at C.J. and Annie. "Witness protection before they testify?" He sneered. "We're going to save the taxpayers the money."

Annie's face went white as winter snow. C.J. handled herself like a pro, Chris decided. She didn't move a muscle. Even her eyes did not betray what she was feeling. Whatever happened in the next few minutes, he knew he could count on her cool head. He would need every advantage possible. He would watch for the right moment to make his move, knowing Nick and C.J. would pick up their cues.

"You, Blondie." Matlock pointed to Annie. "Stuff all those papers into the camera bag."

Terror kept Annie rooted to the spot where she stood. C.J. stepped forward to carry out the order herself. Jennings's hand clamped over her arm, halting her.

"It's all right, Annie," Chris said gently. "Do as he says."

Trembling, Annie inched up to the desk and, with awkward movements, crammed the papers into the bag.

"Zip it closed, then back away from it," Matlock barked.

Annie jumped and yanked the zipper shut. Her eyes were huge in her white face. She was terrified. C.J. gritted her teeth to contain her rage, letting anger block out the fear.

Matlock's smile was pure malevolence. He jerked a pair of handcuffs from his belt and passed them to Jennings.

"You take the bag and the blonde," he told his cohort.

"No," C.J. protested heatedly. She hadn't come this far, hadn't gone through the days of running, of protecting her sister, to give up now. She flashed a glance at Chris, then lunged for her sister.

She heard a scuffle behind her. Annie was only an inch away. C.J. reached her as Jennings slammed the butt of his gun into her own shoulder. Pain shot down her back and arm. She fell to her knees.

"No," Chris shouted. "That's enough."

C.J. responded to the alarm in his voice. She raised her head. Jennings's foot was aimed at her midriff. She rolled to her side. The air whooshed next to her head as he missed her.

Matlock held Chris firmly by the arm, the gun barrel jammed against his temple. She caught the murderous glare Chris threw at Jennings. His expression bore all his fury at his own impotence, at his failure to save her from the blow to her shoulder.

The white-knight syndrome, she thought, and she wasn't a woman to play the damsel in distress for anyone. He was all wrong for her and she for him. In every way that mattered, except for one. But how she wished . . .

"The sheriff's right," Matlock growled. "That's enough. We need all of them to walk out of here."

"Why?" C.J. demanded, her breathing labored.

"We don't want the townspeople to become suspicious."

Chris struggled against Matlock's grip. He wanted to rush to C.J. Seeing Jennings strike her had snapped his control. Matlock pressed the gun harder against his temple.

"That's enough heroics, Sheriff. I'll put a bullet through you if necessary."

"My office is sending more people," Nick warned Matlock. "They already know what's going on with you and Senator Jordainne. And Jennings, here."

Matlock patted his pocket. "I've planned for this day. I've got my ticket out of here. I'll be gone before anyone misses me."

"You won't get away with it," C.J. insisted, getting slowly to her feet.

Matlock gave a derisive snort. "Oh, I will. I know you'll fight me all the way, but in the end, you, and the other three, will be dead. And I'll be out of the country."

"What about me?" Jennings wailed.

Matlock glared disdainfully at the other man. "Don't worry. You'll be taken care of like always. Now let's get out of here. Take the blonde." He stilled C.J. with a sharp glance. "Nothing will happen to her until you're all together again. We're going out to

Riker's place. It's isolated enough for what I have in mind. Let's go.''

C.J. watched helplessly as Jennings jerked Annie's hands behind her back and slapped the handcuffs around her wrists. When he slung the camera bag over his shoulder and turned Annie toward the door, there was fear in her eyes. But there was also an anger and determination that C.J. had seldom seen in her sister. Especially under these circumstances. Where was the panic, the hysteria? She cast one look at C.J. before Jennings propelled her out of the room.

Matlock shoved Chris toward Nick, then gestured to C.J. ''Come on, sweetie,'' he said, grabbing her arm. ''Now, Sheriff, you and the marshal walk nice and easy over to the desk out there. Remember I won't hesitate to shoot her.''

C.J. watched Chris and Nick walk out. Keeping her in front of him, Matlock walked out behind the others. C.J. tried to struggle free, but his grip tightened painfully.

''Hold it,'' he said as they neared the desk. He shoved C.J. toward the desk and pointed to the handcuffs Chris had tossed there earlier. ''Get those.''

She stared at the steel chains. Her stomach knotted. Her heart thudded against her ribs. She wanted to scream in protest against having her hands bound again. She gave Matlock a narrowed glance, measuring her chances of rushing him. The look in his eyes hardened. His stance stiffened.

''Janey,'' Chris said in soft warning.

Janey. She grabbed on to the sound of that, clutched it to her heart to savor during the lonely nights that would follow if they got out of this alive.

She saw the quiet desperation in his eyes, the concern, the trace of fear. This wasn't the time, he was telling her. Matlock had the only weapon. He was a professional. He could get off several rounds, manage one or two direct hits, before she could blink. She breathed to contain her fear.

"Janey," Matlock mocked. "Very touching. Move it."

Chris watched as she slowly reached for the cuffs. Her hand hesitated, shook, then finally she snatched them up. He knew the courage it took for her to follow the command to snap one end around her wrist and the other around Nick's.

"What about me?" Chris asked. He was the only one with two free hands.

"You're driving. We're going to walk out of here looking for all the world as if we've just made a major bust." He grabbed C.J.'s arm and pressed his gun to her rib cage hard enough to make her wince. "I don't have to tell you what happens to her if I shoot her at this close range, do I, Sheriff?"

No. The bullet would explode muscle and tissue, ricochet off bones and pierce vital organs. There would be nothing left of the life, the vibrancy, the laughter and occasional mischief that was C.J. She would be gone. Chris fumed with unbridled fury at the other man. It didn't faze Matlock's smugness. He'd long ago realized Chris wouldn't take any chances with C.J.'s life.

Chris led them out the back door to his Jeep. He had no choice, but just the same, he vowed he would see Matlock in hell before he let him harm C.J. He let her and Nick in the back seat, then got in behind the steering wheel. Matlock got in the passenger side, settling so he had a view of Chris and the two in the back. With mounting trepidation, Chris drove to his house.

Chapter 9

Nightfall would be early. The sky had already darkened. Another round of storm clouds, black and ominous, hung overhead. A cold wind buffeted the Jeep. The weather was announcing the approach of winter as certainly and unfeelingly as Matlock had informed them of their deaths.

"What are your plans for us?" Chris asked.

Matlock's smile was pure malevolence. "Well, Sheriff, there will be a very tragic accident."

"For all four of us?" Chris persisted, meeting C.J.'s gaze in the rearview mirror. She looked back at him with her fear under control and her determination firmly in place. Though it didn't show, he could guess how much she must resent him. She had every right, the way he'd misjudged Matlock's move. He certainly hadn't proven worthy of her trust.

Matlock shrugged. "The original plan was for only

the women to die. But what's an extra couple of bodies?''

"Don't underestimate the intelligence of the people around here," Chris warned. "It won't take them long to figure out this 'accident' was staged."

"I doubt they will, but if they do, or if Talbot's office makes the connection, they'll have to find me to charge me."

"They'll track you down," Nick said firmly.

"The others, maybe," Matlock assured them in an obvious brag. "Jordainne and Jennings don't have the sense to know it's all over. But I knew this day might come. I've been stashing 'retirement' money in a bank. Under an assumed name, of course."

The man was feeling smug now that he figured he had the situation under control. Sure of himself and very talkative, C.J. mused, tightening her fist around the small key in her palm. She needed to play on his cockiness, keep him talking, keep his attention focused on himself.

"Then if you're leaving the country," she said, "why did you bother to hunt us down?"

"Because you and your sister have caused me a lot of grief and I intend to settle the score before I leave."

His voice was cold and emotionless. C.J. pressed on.

"I've heard enough of what you're going to do after we're dead," she snapped, though her voice trembled. "I would rather know what's going to happen to us now."

Her fatalistic words had the desired effect. Matlock laughed heartily. When C.J. squeezed Nick's hand, he glanced at her curiously. She pressed the key into his palm. She felt him go very still for a long moment.

"Yeah, tell us how it's going to happen," he prompted Matlock.

"Simple, but thorough. A dive over a bluff. A crash. We'll make sure there's a gasoline explosion. They'll figure out it's your car, Sheriff, and that you must have been driving, but getting an ID on the other badly burned bodies will take some time."

Put that way, C.J. wished she hadn't brought up the subject. But she had to keep him talking while Nick deftly worked the lock on the cuffs. The car's interior was dark enough that Matlock couldn't see what went on in the back seat. She placed her hand over Nick's wrist to muffle any sound. The soft click went undetected by Matlock, who continued to brag about his unthwartable plan.

"Where is this accident supposed to take place?" Chris asked.

C.J.'s sudden talkative streak made him think something was going on between her and Nick. If he was right, they needed him to keep Matlock's attention occupied—and glean more information concerning their intended demise at the same time. The more they knew about it, the better.

Matlock seemed to consider the question, then decide it couldn't do any harm to tell them. "There's a bluff ten miles or so from your house. A deep ravine. It's dark. You go for a drive to show the ladies the stars. You take a wrong turn." He made a whistling sound to indicate the car plummeting to the depths of the ravine.

Listening to him coldly detail how they were meant to die, C.J.'s stomach clenched sickeningly. Poor Annie, she thought, going through the fear alone. What were they doing to her?

C.J. frowned as another thought occurred to her. "Why did you send Annie with Jennings?"

Matlock chuckled. "Haven't you guessed? Jordainne wants a few minutes alone with her."

C.J. bit her tongue to hold back her hot angry words. "If he touches her..." she ground out.

"You ought to be more concerned over your own fate. You and I have our own score to settle, Janey. You've forced me to step up my retirement plans by several years."

"So sorry Annie and I didn't cooperate the first time you tried to kill us."

"Right about now, I imagine these two gentlemen wish you had."

C.J. swallowed around the lump in her throat. Was that how Chris felt? Did he wish she'd never come into his life? She couldn't blame him. She'd brought him nothing but pain.

But at the moment she needed to concentrate on the here and now. Nick pressed the key to the cuffs into her palm. She closed her fingers around it. She wouldn't risk trying now to unlock the band that cut into her wrist. Nick had his end of the cuffs open. That would give him, and her, a fighting chance.

They would only get the one chance. Matlock was cocky, but he wasn't stupid. And he was armed. She took a deep breath, striving for a cool head as Chris turned the Jeep onto the gravel driveway to his house. Her teeth found her lower lip and tugged mercilessly at the tender skin.

"Slow down," Matlock ordered Chris as the dusky outline of the house came into view.

In the settling darkness the structure loomed large
and sinister as a mausoleum. C.J. shivered. The chill
climbed her spine.

"Stop here," Matlock said.

They were several feet from the house. The lights
were on in the great room downstairs. She saw Chris
gaze in that direction and realized they were thinking
the same thing—that would be where Jordainne had
Annie.

Chris shut off the engine. Matlock took the keys.
He ordered Chris to get out of the car and walk
around the back of the vehicle to open the door for
C.J. and Nick. All the while Matlock kept his gun
trained on them.

C.J. held her breath as Chris opened the door and
stepped back as instructed. Matlock eased out of the
car, then gestured to them. Nick bent his head close to
her ear.

"Fall," was all he whispered to her.

He grasped her hand. In the darkness, that would
be enough to make it appear they were still hand-
cuffed together. He slid his long frame out of the car.
His gaze, like Chris's, was on the man holding the
gun. The two stood braced, watching, ready. That was
C.J.'s cue. She stepped out of the Jeep, and fell.

She hit the ground hard. Nick dropped her hand.
He and Chris lunged for Matlock. C.J. rolled aside.
She heard the sound of fist striking flesh, once, twice.
Then shouts from the house. And gunshots. Trembling, she got to her knees. Someone grabbed her arm
and pulled her around the Jeep. Her stomach knotted
as a bullet grazed the roof and ricocheted.

"Stay down," Chris commanded. His fingers still dug into her upper arm. "Did you get his gun?" he asked Nick.

"It flew out of his hand when you hit him. I couldn't find it."

The man on the deck aimed a volley of bullets at the Jeep. Chris pulled C.J. against his chest, shielding her with his body. The man on the deck stopped to reload.

Chris motioned to Nick. "Those trees. Away from the light." He pulled C.J. to her feet. They ran across the gravel driveway. "How the hell did you two get loose?" he demanded once they were all behind a large tree trunk.

"She had the damn key, man," Nick said in an amazed whisper.

C.J. drew in a ragged breath, the first full breath she'd taken since seeing Matlock holding a gun on Chris. "You threw it on the desk right next to the cuffs. I palmed it when I picked them up."

"I like a woman who's always thinking," Nick declared.

Chris didn't answer. C.J. wished she knew what he was thinking, how he felt about her. But her questions would have to wait.

"Riker."

He whirled around at the sound of his name. The shout came from the deck. She peered around the tree. There were three figures on the deck. Matlock, Jennings and Annie.

C.J. gasped. Annie was alive, but she was a long way from being safe. Her hands were still cuffed behind her. Matlock had his arm around her middle.

C.J. didn't realize she'd instinctively moved toward her sister until Chris tugged her back behind the tree.

"We have to stay cool," he cautioned her. "I'd hoped I hit the bastard hard enough he wouldn't come to."

"Riker," Matlock shouted once more. "I know you can hear me. We've still got the sister." He shoved Annie to the railing and pressed a gun to her temple. "You understand me, Riker? I'll kill her."

C.J. bit her lip to keep from crying out. She couldn't give away their position, but she couldn't stand by and do nothing while Matlock hurt her sister.

"Give it up, Riker. You can't get far on foot. I've got the keys to your Jeep. There's no one around for miles." He tightened his arm around his prisoner. The wind carried Annie's cry of pain to the trees. "I know you won't go anywhere without her. We'll be waiting for you to make a move." He shoved Annie inside the house.

"We have to get to her," C.J. whispered desperately to Chris.

He gripped her shoulders tightly. "We will. I swear."

There was an edge to his voice she'd never heard before, biting and cold as the north wind blowing through the hills. Whatever had to be done to save them, he would do.

"Matlock won't hurt her," he continued. "He's using her as bait to lure us inside."

"Surely he knows we won't surrender," she protested.

"He knows. He also knows we'll try to get Annie out. That's what he's waiting for."

"Then what do we do?" C.J. asked, leaning into his embrace. The power of his hands, the faint scent of him, his hard muscles pressed against her. A safe haven. A strong fortress. Too late she'd realized how much she needed that, needed him.

C.J. was giving him her trust, Chris realized as he held her. He only hoped he could live up to it this time. The odds were not in his favor. Three, possibly four, armed and trained men against two equally well-trained but unarmed men and two women.

"Let's get closer to the house," he said.

He caught her wrist and felt the steel band encircling it. At the thought of what Matlock had put her through, his rage burned even deeper.

"Give me the key," he said.

When she did, he quickly unlocked the cuffs and looped them through his belt. He would use them on Matlock. This time he would take care of the FBI man for good.

He took her hand in his and, with Nick close behind, led her through the trees that lined the driveway. A few yards from the rear corner of the house, he stopped.

"You stay here." He situated her behind another thick trunk.

Panic rocked through C.J. at the thought of being left alone. "Wait," she said as he turned toward Nick. "Where are you going?"

"To try and find out how many of them there are, and make sure they don't have someone outside looking for us." When her breath caught at the last part, Chris rushed to reassure her. "I don't think they do. They'll want us inside, where there's less chance of our getting away."

"But—"

"We don't have time. Nick and I can do this quicker on our own. Just promise me you'll stay here. As dark as it is, if you don't make any noise, someone could walk past you and never know you were here."

"He's right," Nick put in.

C.J. breathed deeply. "Okay," she said, exhaling slowly, and praying for enough courage and calm to do as he asked. "Just . . . be careful."

As Chris got up, his foot kicked something on the ground. He reached down and picked up the section of a branch, about three feet long, several inches around and solid. Not the weapon he would prefer to leave C.J. with, but it was better than nothing. He thrust it into her hands.

"If you have to use it," he instructed, "swing hard and put all your weight behind it."

"How will I know if it's you coming back?"

He whistled a birdcall. "I'll do that twice."

He and Nick got to their feet and turned toward the house. The shadows swallowed them, leaving C.J. alone with her thoughts and fears.

She strained to hear beyond nature's night noises, but all she heard were the crickets and the occasional cry of an owl in the distance. Life sounds. Oddly out of place now with killers in Chris's house.

Annie would be terrified. What were they doing to her? She'd trusted C.J. to keep her safe through this whole ordeal, and C.J. had let her down, had let everyone down, had placed the people she loved in extreme danger.

Crouching on the ground, she breathed deeply once more and prayed that Chris would be all right. She had longed to demand to go with him, but she'd deferred to his judgment and expertise.

And to his wishes. His need to have her safe generated a range of unfamiliar feelings. While she chafed at being left behind, his protectiveness made her feel cherished. She'd never had anyone to look out for her. But was Chris doing it because he cared for her? Could it be that, despite everything, he still felt something for her?

Chris. Where was he? She stood, determined to find him. He might need her help— No. He could take care of himself. He'd said as much in his office. Her heart heavy, she forced herself to remain where she was and wait. And wait and wait.

To keep the fear at bay, she listened intently to the sounds carried on the wind, trying to pick out one that would indicate he was coming back to her. The wind whined. The leaves rustled loudly. An owl hooted again in the distant darkness. The eerie sound made C.J. shiver.

Then she heard it. The soft crunch of dried leaves being crushed underfoot. A sniff. Her heart pummeled her rib cage. She held her breath. Squeezed her eyes shut. Willed herself into rigid stillness. She heard the sound again. Closer. Coming toward her. She wouldn't scream, wouldn't faint. Closer. Close. She prayed for the sound of Chris's birdcall. It didn't come.

Gripping the piece of log, she got to her feet and braced herself against the tree trunk. She would wait until he came around the tree. One step. Another. A shuffle. Suddenly he was beside her. He threw his weight against her leg. Stunned at the sudden lunge, C.J. wobbled. She dropped the log as she grabbed for balance. Something wet brushed the back of her hand, followed by the swipe of a tongue across her skin.

Charlemagne. C.J. wanted to scream at the animal for scaring her to death, to shout with relief because she wasn't alone. But she didn't dare make a sound. She threw her arms around the dog's neck, grateful Chris had let the creature run free today. A canine companion was better than none.

"Where's Chris?" she whispered. "I bet you could take me right to him, couldn't you, fella?"

Her mind had conjured up horrible scenarios of him in deadly trouble. The man she loved was in danger. She had to do something. . . .

She pulled her resolve together and straightened. The dog nosed around on the ground, startled some small creature into running, then gave chase. C.J. was alone again. Alone and afraid. She hadn't heard any shouts or shots, but it seemed like hours since Chris had left her waiting in the darkness. She gripped the branch tightly. Which way had he gone? Had he and Nick split up?

If only there was a moon, or at least an occasional flash of lightning to break the darkness. But the storm was still too far away. Thunder grumbled quietly over the hills. The wind moaned. Then she heard it. A bird. A pause. Then a second short chirp. The breath she'd held rushed out as she made out the shape of Chris's wide shoulders. Nick was behind him.

"Thank God," she whispered as they came up to her. Chris was safe. She longed to run her hand over him to reassure herself he was really there and was unhurt, longed to beg him to take her in his arms, wrap her in his strength and caring. But she'd lost that right. He stood close, but didn't reach for her.

Chris had heard her relieved sigh when he showed up. He wanted to hold her, to reassure her, but he held back. He'd made all the first moves in their relationship and it had earned him nothing. He wanted some sign from her that she needed him.

"What did you find out?" she asked urgently.

The hope he'd held on to died a little at her question. "There's only the one car. The one Jennings drove out here," he said. "So chances are good there's only three of them inside, four counting the gunman that was on the deck."

Not impossible odds, C.J. thought. "But they have guns and we don't. And you said they'll be waiting for us to make a move."

"We'll have to be sneakier than they expect," Nick stated. "But we'd better get moving."

"We'll have to get in through the dog door." Chris laid a hand lightly on C.J.'s shoulder. He didn't want to put her in direct danger, but there was no other way to get into the house without being detected. "Hopefully they never noticed it was there. You're the only one small enough to get through it." He led them to the shadows at the side of the house.

He was asking for her help because he had no choice, C.J. had to acknowledge. She was ridiculously clinging to hope, wishing he might give her a chance to prove they could work out the problems between them. She pressed her back against the house.

"What do I do?" she asked in a strained whisper.

"While you explain," Nick interrupted, "I'll get in place." He turned and disappeared into the darkness.

"He's going to a window on the other side," Chris said before she could ask. "He'll give us time for you to crawl through the cutout and open the door for me."

"Then what?"

"We try to get upstairs while he sets up a distraction at the window."

Divide and conquer. Sounded easy enough, she supposed, wiping her damp palms on the legs of her jeans. Someone would go to investigate the commotion Nick made, possibly leaving only one man guarding Annie.

"But first," he told her, "let's get inside."

He was right. One thing at a time. C.J. got down on her knees before the cutout. "Will it creak?"

"Charlie works the hinges enough to keep them operating smoothly." He listened at the door. "I don't hear anyone. And Nick should be ready. Squeeze through, then reach up and turn the handle."

She nodded. Chris pushed the cutout open and held it for her. With a deep breath, C.J. ducked her head and crawled through. The cement floor was cold as death under her palms. The wood frame scraped against her shoulders, her ankles. The blackness of the night was even denser inside. The dark closed around her like a shroud. She shivered at the direction of her thoughts.

"The knob," Chris whispered urgently once she was inside.

She shoved her morbid thoughts aside and felt for the knob, closed both hands around it, then slowly turned it. The quiet click reverberated in her ears, but there was no sound from upstairs. Chris silently opened the door and eased inside. When he put his arms around her and pressed her to his solid chest, C.J. realized she was trembling.

"It's okay." Chris tucked her head under his chin. Though he knew it was best to be emotionally detached, he couldn't manage it. He needed to give C.J. what comfort he could, needed to feel her lean on him, cling to him, if only for this brief moment. "We're almost there," he said, though the worst was still ahead of them.

C.J. nodded, strengthened by the tiny contact with him. His breathing was even and controlled. She steadied her own to match his. She needed a clear head and the calm that came with it. "I'm sorry," she whispered.

"Sorry?"

She nodded. This wasn't the time to go into apologies and confessions, but she was realistic enough to know she might not get another chance.

"I screwed up royally," she muttered. "It wasn't supposed to happen this way."

In her plans Annie was supposed to be with her, not alone and scared senseless. Being caught in Matlock's trap was not part of the plan, either. Nor was involving other people—no matter how well trained they were for this type of situation. And she'd certainly never intended to fall in love. But she had and there wasn't a damned thing she could do about it.

"C.J.," Chris began. There was so much he wanted to tell her, but his tumultuous thoughts and emotions refused to sort themselves out in the short instant allowed him.

"I know," she told him. "We don't have time. What do you want me to do?"

She was right, Chris knew. If they didn't make it through this mess alive, it would be pointless to worry about sorting out his feelings. If they survived, C.J.

would walk out of his life. Both ways, he lost. Squaring his shoulders, he took her hand and led her to the shelves along the far wall. He pressed a wrench into her hand.

"A weapon," he said. "We'll get into the kitchen. From there we ought to be able to see where they have Annie."

He felt around on the shelf and came up with a crowbar. "Let's go. Nick must be ready."

As if on cue, the floor upstairs creaked. Footsteps scrambled across the great room floor toward the west window.

Chris pulled her toward the stairs, holding her hand as they silently made their way up the stairs and into the darkened kitchen, one slow heart-pounding step after the other. C.J. crouched beside him, their backs to the cabinets. He could feel the tension radiate from her taut body. He squeezed her cold hand in silent reassurance. She looked up at him with eyes wide with fear.

"I told you this was a stupid idea," a male voice shouted in the great room.

"Shut up, Jordainne," Matlock growled.

"This makes twice you've screwed up."

"As usual, you've conveniently forgotten who the hell got us into this in the first place."

Chris glanced at C.J. again. The best time to move would be now while Matlock and Jordainne argued. He motioned for her to follow him to the kitchen doorway.

"It's her fault," Jordainne insisted.

Chris ventured a peek into the other room. The senator pointed to Annie. She sat, hands behind her back, in the chair nearest the fireplace. Her face was chalk white. There was blood on her lower lip. Chris heard Matlock laugh bitterly, saw him shove Jordainne's hand away.

"That's it, always blame it on the bimbo," he snarled at the senator.

Both men had their backs to the kitchen. Matlock had a gun, Chris knew. The senator didn't seem the type to carry a weapon, but that was no guarantee he was unarmed now. A crowbar was no match for bullets. He would have to get closer and hope the element of surprise would give him the edge he needed.

By now Nick should have subdued the man who'd gone after him and should be making his way to the basement. Chris debated waiting for him, then decided he'd better make his move now while Jordainne and Matlock stood only a foot apart. He could take them both out—

The front door burst open. In a breath, Chris sank back into the shadows of the kitchen. He plastered himself against the cabinets and gestured for C.J. to do the same.

"Get inside," a man ordered.

"Take it easy, Jennings," Nick said loudly.

C.J.'s breath caught. Jennings had Nick. Perspiration dotted her forehead. Her palms were wet, but she didn't dare try to wipe them, afraid any movement would give them away. She molded her spine to the wood and gripped the wrench with painful tightness.

Chris peered around the doorjamb. There were two men escorting Nick down the short hall toward the great room. Chris waited until the group was even with him, then lunged for the two men behind his friend.

C.J. gasped as Chris propelled himself through the doorway, swinging the crowbar. He hit the first man—

Jennings, she realized—but the second man dived at Chris. C.J. was dimly aware that Nick charged at the two men in the great room. Her attention was on Chris, wrestling with the other man. He landed a blow on Chris's square jaw, dazing him. The man raised his fist again.

C.J. lurched to her feet, gripping the wrench with both hands and praying she had the guts to do what needed to be done. She'd never struck anyone. But the man had Chris pinned to the floor.

She swung the wrench at the man's head a second too late. He twisted. The wrench glanced off his shoulder. She brought her arm back to swing again. Jennings grabbed her from behind. Hot pain seered through her wrist as he twisted it. The wrench clattered to the floor. He jerked her arm behind her back. C.J. bit her lip to keep from crying out.

"Hold it, Sheriff," Jennings ground out. "I'll break her arm."

Chris whirled to face him. He had C.J.'s arm bent at a painful angle. Chris released his hold on the man who'd come in with Jennings.

"No," C.J. said through clenched teeth. "Chris, don't stop—"

Jennings gave her arm a vicious yank. She gasped. Her eyes filled with tears of pain, but she didn't cry out. That was the second time Jennings had hurt her. Chris vowed he would settle the score personally.

"Get up slowly, Sheriff," Jennings ordered, jabbing a gun barrel into C.J.'s side.

Chris measured his chances of rushing Jennings. The man's hands shook. His eyes darted nervously from Chris to C.J. His reaction time would be slowed by his own fear.

"Don't try it, Riker," Matlock said from the great room doorway.

Chris turned. Matlock had his gun trained on Nick. There was nothing Chris could do at the moment. He got to his feet. The man he'd hit ran a hand under his nose, studied the blood on his hand, then got up.

"In the other room," he growled, shoving Chris in that direction.

They filed into the great room. Jennings waited until the others were lined up in front of the fireplace before he released C.J. She rushed to her sister's side. Annie's lip was bleeding. The beginnings of a bruise showed on her cheekbone.

"You snake," C.J. hissed at Jordainne.

The crystal-blue eyes that had mesmerized female voters across the country glittered with malice. "I would have done more," the senator snarled, "if Jennings hadn't stopped me."

"We don't want blood in the house, or anything else that might make someone wonder if their accident was not so accidental," Jennings pointed out.

"I've already told my office about you and your network," Nick supplied.

"But without proof to back you up," Jordainne said with a grin, "it's all supposition. The men I work for will kill the nasty rumors just like they've taken care of everything else that might get in the way of my being elected the next president of the United States."

He walked over to the coffee table. The camera bag sat on one end, the evidence spread out next to it. C.J.'s eyes narrowed as he placed the papers in the fireplace, took out a cigarette lighter and touched the flame to them. She watched the fire creep along the edges of the papers, thinking of the inferno planned for them.

"I made copies," C.J. said.

For an instant Jordainne looked frightened, then he shook his head. "I don't believe you. We searched your apartment in D.C., and went through your car and through that hotel room. There are no copies."

C.J. turned her gaze to Matlock. He sneered at the senator's back. Jordainne was clueless enough to believe burning that set of papers would solve everything. Matlock might suspect C.J. really had hidden other copies somewhere safe, but with his one-way ticket out of the country, why should he bother to warn Jordainne?

Chris caught Nick's glance. Jordainne stared at the fire. Matlock glared at his back. Jennings's attention, and the fourth man's, was divided between Jordainne and their prisoners. Now was the time to move. Chris nodded to Nick.

Chris dived for Matlock, throwing his weight at the agent's thick middle. They fell to the floor with a bone-jarring thud. Nick ducked like a linebacker and tackled Jennings and the other man. They all went down, but Nick couldn't handle two men alone for long.

C.J. looked around for a weapon and spotted the camera bag. She reached for it just as Jordainne grabbed her wrist. His grip was powerful. She wrestled to break his hold, but his hand only tightened. She gritted her teeth against the pain. The harder he pulled, the harder she struggled against him. But she knew she was losing ground. She could hear the others still fighting. Then she heard Annie.

Hands still bound behind her back, she charged at Jordainne, broadsiding him. The impact knocked him over. He pulled C.J. down with him. Her head grazed the corner of the coffee table. Pain spiked through her. Her body went limp. She fought against the blackness. She couldn't pass out.

She raised to one elbow. Jordainne had released her to deal with Annie, who was furiously kicking at his body. C.J. fumbled around the top of the table until her hand landed on the camera bag strap. She pulled the equipment toward her. The zoom lens was the first thing she grabbed.

Holding it in one hand, she crawled toward Jordainne. He was so busy defending himself from Annie's assault, he didn't notice her. Long past being afraid, C.J. gripped the lens firmly, raised it and brought it down on Jordainne's head with all her strength. She raised her weapon, prepared to strike again. But Jordainne didn't move. Bright red blood oozed through the strands of his blond hair.

Annie gasped. Her eyes widened. "You knocked him out."

"Serves him right," C.J. grumbled around the pounding in her head.

She took a breath and turned to see how Chris and Nick fared. One man was down for the count, but they were still fighting—Chris with Jennings and Nick with Matlock. Though she wasn't quite steady on her feet yet, she tightened her hold on the lens.

"Sit on him," she told Annie. "If he wakes up, kick him some more and yell for help."

Annie gulped, then nodded. Chris seemed to have the upper hand with Jennings, but continued to pummel the man mercilessly. C.J. advanced on Nick and

Matlock. She had a score or two she wanted to settle with the FBI man, as well.

She studied the pair carefully. They twisted and turned on the floor, trading blows. Somehow she would have to get close enough to clobber Matlock without getting trampled in the fracas.

Finally the moment came. Matlock landed a solid punch on his opponent's jaw. Nick shook his head dazedly. C.J. raised the zoom lens. Matlock caught hold of Nick's vest. He pulled his arm back just as Nick recovered. He blocked the blow. With what appeared to be superhuman strength, he hit Matlock. The man's arm flew back, connecting with C.J.'s jaw. She heard sirens. Light filled the room. Then everything went black.

Someone slapped her cheeks. C.J. came to enough to know that her head was about to explode.

"Oh, God," Annie wailed. "She can't be dead. She's got to be all right. C.J...."

There was noise all around. Voices. Footsteps. The pounding in her head. C.J. tried to open her eyes. Light speared her head. She groaned.

"Is she coming around?" Annie asked. "Does this mean she's going to be okay? Please let her be okay."

"Get a grip," C.J. managed weakly.

Something painfully cold was placed on her head. Ice. She tried to shove it away.

"No, Janey. It's an ice pack. I know it doesn't feel good now, but it'll help the pain."

Chris's voice. Crooning to her. Calling her Janey again. Oh, how wonderful to hear the warmth behind the words.

She worked to get her eyes open. She had to see his face, had to see the warmth in his eyes. But by the time her eyes had adjusted to the light in the room, he was gone. It was Annie's worried face that she saw. Tears streaked down her cheeks.

"You hit your head on the floor," she said. "I thought you'd never wake up."

"Where's Chris?" C.J. asked, afraid she already knew the answer.

"Helping one of his deputies get Jordainne loaded into a car. You really cracked his skull. The worm still hasn't come to."

Holding the ice pack on the bump on her head, C.J. chanced a cautious look around. There were people everywhere, some in jeans, others in dark government-regulation suits, still others in sheriffs' uniforms. Even Charlemagne had shown up to see what was going on. The dog stood beside the deputy guarding Jennings, growling menacingly at the pair.

"Chris told me you don't like the gun," the deputy crooned to the animal. "But you'll just have to put up with it for a while, fella. Just until we get the trash cleaned out of here."

Everyone seemed to be in on the act. Everyone except Chris. He'd left as soon as he knew she was going to come to. She'd mistaken the concern she'd heard in his voice. Perhaps she'd even imagined that he'd called her Janey. But there was one thing she wasn't imagining. He was gone.

Chapter 10

Chris surveyed his office. The news that Sen. Alex Jordainne was behind bars in the local jail had spread like a lightning fire through summer-dried brush.

Once Sam and Willie had found and revived Oliver, they'd contacted the volunteer snow-removal crew, made them unofficial deputies and assigned them to help comb the area to find Chris and his friends. Or prisoners. Oliver hadn't been sure how to classify C.J. and her sister since Chris had arrested them hours before.

C.J. He glanced across the room to where she sat, huddled in her jacket, still shivering, her face lined with the aftermath of tension and fear. Annie was beside her. The two of them were surrounded by federal marshals and what passed for the local press. Then there were the men on the snow crew who were enjoying the thrill of being in the thick of things for once. Add to that the handful of curious townspeople who stood around, holding up walls and sitting on desks and generally adding to the confusion.

Chris had given the newspaper editor a brief statement, but still he'd been forced to tell and retell how Jordainne's criminal activities had come to light. Even in remote Wyoming, the senator was well-known and liked. Accepting that his reputation was a carefully manufactured facade wasn't easy for any of them. Everyone wanted to hear the story, and they all seemed determined to approach Chris individually for the details.

It was standing room only in this three-ring circus, and he was the ringmaster. All he wanted to do was demand that everyone get the hell out and leave him alone. Unfortunately that was the one thing he couldn't do. So much had happened between him and C.J., and it had all happened so fast he hadn't had time to sort through his feelings.

He'd fallen in love with her, had thought she might love him in return, only to discover she would rather take her chances alone than confide in him. He'd never been as furious with anyone as he'd been with her. Or as devastated. How could he still want to spend the rest of his life with her? Yet he couldn't get her out of his system. He couldn't let her go, but he couldn't make her stay.

Moot point, he told himself. It appeared C.J. had already decided she didn't need him in her life. She hadn't spoken to him since she came to after Jordainne hit her. The few times their gazes had met, she'd quickly looked away.

He should face the facts and get on with his life.

"Sheriff?"

Pulled out of his unpleasant reflections, Chris scowled down at his deputy.

"You look like you're gonna kill someone," Sam said. "You okay?"

"Fine," Chris answered without much conviction. He turned away from the sight of the woman he loved, looking unapproachable, surrounded by a throng of people. Her welfare was not his concern any longer. If it ever had been. "You want something, Sam?"

The young deputy shrugged. "The senator..."

"He still screaming about his constitutional rights?"

"Yeah, that, too. His lawyer's on the phone. How do you want to handle it?"

Chris would have preferred to take the phone to Jordainne, but there was no phone jack downstairs. He swore under his breath. If the place was a madhouse now, it would be even worse when Sam marched Jordainne upstairs.

"The good senator will have to use my office," Chris said. "Take Willie with you when you go for him. Cuff him before you let him out of the cell."

Extreme precautions, maybe, but Chris wasn't taking any chances. He couldn't forget that Jordainne and Matlock had plotted to kill C.J., that they'd come very close to succeeding. It wasn't a lot, and she probably wouldn't appreciate it, but Chris would give her all the protection he could before she was gone from his life.

C.J. didn't know anything could hurt so much. Each time Chris looked at her with his icy, expressionless gaze, she died a little inside. She had hoped there might be something left of what they'd shared, but her mistrust had killed the fire, down to the very last ember. She couldn't deny reality when it stared at her with eyes colder than death.

As Annie came to the end of her rambling tale of how she'd brought down the senator from Pennsylvania, C.J. stole a glance at Chris's broad back, rigid, unyielding.

"C.J.?" Annie tugged at her sleeve.

C.J. realized Chris had gone into his office with Jordainne and one of the deputies. She'd been staring at the closed door, willing him to rush out and take her in his arms. But the door never opened.

"C.J.?" Annie repeated, watching her curiously.

C.J. tore her gaze away from the door.

"I'll take you back to the hotel to get your things," Nick said.

So it was over. The running. The endless terror. And a love rare and wonderful beyond words. Weary in body and spirit, she reached for her camera bag and slung the strap over her shoulder.

"Aren't you..." Annie pointed to Chris's closed office door. "Don't you want to..."

C.J. shook her head. There was nothing left to say. She looked up at Nick and resolutely squared her shoulders. "Let's go."

There were two cars outside and more federal marshals. She and Annie were escorted to Nick's car. But not even Annie's chatter could distract C.J. from thoughts of the man she was leaving behind.

Saying goodbye to Chris wouldn't have changed things between them, she told herself repeatedly. He was most likely glad she was gone. She'd caused him nothing but grief and had very nearly gotten him killed. No, a final farewell wouldn't have changed a thing.

Chris pulled the Jeep onto the grassy shoulder and shut off the engine. The landscape stretched on as far as the eye could see—scattered patches of pine trees, softly sloping hills and acres of grazing land. The morning sun shone down on it all, but without any warmth. C.J. had taken that with her when she left his office last night.

He hadn't intended to come here, to the place where he'd first seen her, standing by the rusted red car and looking slender and sexy enough to tempt a man to sin. He could still remember the way her fascinating eyes had gazed back at him with cautious awareness, could remember the lilt of her voice, and could remember how quickly he'd fallen for her.

If he let her leave Redman, there would be no peace for him here in Wyoming any longer. The ghosts would be everywhere, and as if not having her there with him wouldn't be torture enough, he would think of her every time he revisited each place they'd been. The wound would never heal. He would keep picking at the scab, making it bleed time and again. But the painful memories wouldn't bring her back.

Alone in his bed last night, he'd ached for her. From now on, each time he stopped at Shari's diner for lunch or dinner, he would remember C.J. sitting across the table from him. He might even take one of Bill Hawks's horses and ride back to the hillside where he'd first made love to her.

None of it would bring her back. He twisted the key in the ignition and resolutely drove back to his office.

"Fax for you," Sam informed him the minute he walked in.

Chris glanced absently at the paper, then realized the letter was from Nick. He took it into his office and sat behind the desk to read it.

Nick figured the wealthy and powerful men named in Jordainne's papers wouldn't pose a great threat to C.J. or her sister. Those men had the country's top legal talent at their disposal, and Jordainne's papers alone wouldn't be enough to send them to prison. Jordainne, however, had other more incriminating evidence against them. Nick hoped the prosecutor could convince Jordainne to turn state's evidence. Jennings was already spilling his guts to try to save his hide.

The biggest threat to C.J. and Annie would come from Matlock, but he'd been booked and denied bail. He would soon be behind bars for good. Everything had been wrapped up in a nice neat package.

"Everything except my feelings for C.J.," Chris muttered.

C.J. took one last look out the hotel window. Tomorrow she would be a million miles from Redman, Wyoming. A million miles from a horizon that stretched on forever, from air full of nature's scents. A lifetime from the only man who had aroused her passion and awakened her senses beyond anything she'd ever dreamed. The only man who had made her soul sing.

After Nick had left her at the hotel, she'd stayed up the rest of the night using the sink and tub in the bathroom to develop some of the photos she'd taken of Chris. Now she could feel his presence all around her. Everywhere she turned in this small bedroom, she came face-to-face with his essence captured forever on film. Laughing. Smiling. The gleam in his eyes sparkling back at her. For her. She could reach out for the man she loved.

But the only thing she touched was a cold, lifeless photograph of him. There were a dozen of them, spread out over the narrow bed. Chris's face. His every expression. Never changing. Haunting her.

He was there with her. But only in memory. Each photo was a painful reminder of all she'd shared with him. Of all she'd had and lost.

No amount of time would dull the pain. If the past few hours were any indication, time would only make the aching loneliness worse. An eternity without his love. Never to see him smile at her. Never to hear the sound of his voice. Never to know the rapture of making love with him again. He'd shown her heaven, and she'd condemned herself to hell. Without Chris, she would always be empty inside.

He'd been there for her every step of the awful nightmare with Jordainne. He'd protected her and had saved her life. He'd made her fall in love with him. If only she'd realized that before it was too late.

C.J. picked up one of the photos and traced the outline of his face. She could imagine him so easily. Just wish for him and he would come alive in her mind. Like now. In the doorway. Just a few steps away. Dressed in his uniform, his hat in his hands. So real she could hear the whisper of his breath, read the pain in his forest-green eyes.

Haunted eyes that spoke of a loneliness as deep and abiding as her own. An emptiness of spirit and soul where there had been laughter and contentment. And love.

How could that be? She frowned at the specter who advanced a step into the room and stopped. She wanted to remember him gazing down at her with hunger and love. She didn't want to recall the pain she'd caused him, didn't want to think he might be suffering.

She blinked to hold back the tears that filled her eyes. God, how she ached for him, for his laughter and his love. For the peace and joy she'd found with him.

If only the vision of him in the doorway were real. She looked down at the photo in her hand.

Chris followed her gaze from the one print she held to the others that covered the bed. She didn't seem to believe he was here. She hadn't looked at him so much as through him.

As if she thought she was dreaming. But he'd seen the pain and wistfulness in her eyes. His gut tightened. He hadn't counted on her being miserable. She'd gone through so much, carried a lot of weight on those slender shoulders. Adding to her burdens was not what he wanted. Her pain cut through to his soul.

His averted gaze landed on the black-and-white prints spread over the bed. All of them were of him. Her camera had captured his every emotion. Then he saw the open suitcase on the other bed. The clothes inside the case were neatly packed. She was leaving.

They still had a lot of things to work out. This morning he'd decided he couldn't let her go until they'd at least talked.

"You never said goodbye," he growled. How could she think of walking out without a backward glance as if nothing had happened between them?

She gasped. Her eyes wide, she stared at him. Shock. Surprise. Joy. Then uncertainty and fear. The expressions flitted across her lovely face in the blink of an eye, but Chris felt them all.

"You really *are* here," she said in a whisper. "I'm not imagining. . . ."

He nodded, unable to find his voice.

C.J. continued to stare at him for a long moment. "Why. . ."

Her voice cracked on the word. She hadn't dared to hope he might still care. But he hadn't said anything about caring, she warned her heart before it could run completely away with happiness.

He must have some last-minute business, she decided, clamping the lid on the hopes that had sprung to life the instant she realized the figure in the doorway was flesh and blood and not merely a product of her need.

"We have to talk." Chris was desperately trying to hold back the need to have her in his arms, to feel her soft body pressed against the length of him. He couldn't let his emotions overrule logic and reason again.

C.J. scooped up the photos and gestured for him to sit on the edge of the bed. She carefully laid the prints on the suitcase, then turned back to him. Her heart pounded a painful erratic rhythm against her ribs. There was so much she wanted to tell him that she couldn't find words for any of it. All she could think about was the pain in his eyes. Pain that she'd caused. Did he still hate her? He had every right.

"I'm sorry," she said quietly. "I never meant for things to turn out this way."

"What things?" he demanded, his eyes going cold again.

C.J.'s heartbeat faltered. "Us."

The word hung in the air between them, another block in the wall she'd begun building with her mistrust. A dividing wall between them. Was there any way to scale it, to break through it? Or was it there to stay, a permanent barrier between them?

"Us," he repeated tonelessly.

Chris squeezed the brim of his hat with a force he could barely control. She was sorry about them. About all they'd shared, about the love they'd made. About the only truly beautiful thing that had come out of this entire situation.

"I guess we don't have anything to talk about, after all." He started to get to his feet.

"Please," she begged, dropping her hand on his arm. He tensed. Her touch brought back more of the wonderful memories, memories that he couldn't bury, memories that she regretted. And still he yearned for her, ached to feel her hands on him as they made love. How could she have him this mixed up, his emotions in total turmoil?

"I never should have come." He yanked his arm free and started toward the door.

C.J. rushed across the room. She couldn't let him leave, had to make him hear her out. She shoved the door closed and pressed her back to the wood, blocking his exit. He glared down at her. A muscle in his jaw knotted. She was no match for him, she knew. If he really wanted to leave, he could easily pick her up and set her out of his way. He looked as though he was considering that very thing, but then he turned away, obviously struggling for control.

C.J. spotted the handcuffs hanging from his belt. Desperate times . . . She snatched one end of the cuffs and clamped the band around her wrist.

"What the . . ." he sputtered.

She pulled the cuffs free from his belt, and as he whirled around to face her, she clamped the other end around his wrist. His eyes narrowed.

"Don't bother going for your keys," she warned him.

His mouth opened, but the words didn't come right away. "What do you think you're doing?" he finally managed.

"You were right, we do need to talk. This way neither one of us can run away before everything is said and done."

He stared suspiciously at the band binding him to her. "C.J.," he said.

"We're both good at running," she rushed to say. "Except for my family and my one early failure at romance, I've perfected the art of bailing out of relationships when things began to get serious."

"Then what's so different about this time?"

Did she detect a small softening in his attitude? She breathed deeply and forged ahead. She had to make him understand, make him see that she had cared, that she still did. This would be her last chance.

"You," she said. "You're what makes this time different. Because no matter how many miles we put between us, you'll always be with me."

There was a vulnerability in her eyes Chris couldn't ignore. It called to the part of him that lived only to cherish and love her. He wanted to believe she was breaking down the barriers, baring her soul to him at last. But he'd been wrong about her once before. He'd thought that when she had his love, she would give him her trust. It hadn't happened. Instead she'd smashed his heart and left it in a thousand shattered pieces.

"Why should I believe you?" he demanded, forcing himself to stand firm against his traitorous longing to take her and make love to her again and again. For now and for the rest of his life.

C.J. wanted him so badly, but she was scared to death. If he said he didn't love her, her world would crash down around her. She hadn't understood when her mother had tried to explain how one man could become so important that a woman would do anything, give up anything, endure any hardship, just to be with him. Looking into the eyes she would never forget, C.J. understood.

Had she screwed up everything between them? She had to know. She squared her shoulders, raised her chin and took the biggest risk of her life.

"I love you." She'd said it. The words were out in the open now. He could take them and she would belong to him for the rest of her life. Or he could leave them. And leave her.

Chris wanted to believe her, more than he wanted to go on breathing. The truth was he needed her. Without her, life would be intolerably empty, a darkness with no end. But he needed more than just her love. This time he had to lead with his head, not his hormones.

"In my book, love and trust go hand in hand," he said.

C.J. let out the breath she'd been holding. She wasn't in the clear yet, she knew. She had a lot to answer for, but at least he was going to listen. She wanted to throw herself into his warm embrace, but she had to earn that right.

She led him back to the narrow bed, sitting on one side while he sat on the other. She ran a fingertip over the cold steel encircling her wrist.

"Prisoner of love," she murmured.

"Is that the way you see it?"

The coldness was back in his voice. C.J. looked up at him. This time she didn't try to hide her feelings, her fear and her hopes.

"In a way. Love is scary, chancy. It sneaks up when you're not looking. And it's demanding—all or nothing. You and I, we'd known each other for four days when we made love on that hillside, but I couldn't have stopped you, or stopped myself." She breathed deeply, hoping she could make him understand. "I know I lied about other things, but I never lied about my feelings for you."

He was silent for a long moment. "Then why didn't you trust me?" he asked finally.

"I did, deep inside. But I was afraid. There was so much at stake. My life. Annie's. That evening, after we made love at your house, I wanted to tell you everything. I started to. I really did."

"What stopped you?"

"Nick's call. You said he was with the U.S. Marshals Office and I was afraid all over again. Scared you knew, scared he was coming to take me and Annie back to D.C., scared you wouldn't believe me."

His expression hardened again.

"I know I made a major mistake, but try to see it from my perspective. We'd taken the evidence to one FBI agent and he'd cut a hole in my car's brake lines."

He could have lost her, Chris thought, angry at the man who'd tried to kill her. Matlock might have succeeded and then Chris would never have known her. He would have spent the rest of his life without her.

Sitting here, looking into her blue-gray eyes, his mouth went dry and he couldn't remember a damned thing other than how empty he felt without her.

Need crowded out the words he struggled to form. Need to love her and be loved by her. How to tell her what was in his heart when she was the most important thing in his life.

She was biting her lower lip. He touched a finger to her mouth, gently tracing the spot she'd bitten.

"I haven't been able to get you off my mind," he said softly.

Her eyes widened. He heard her breath catch. It was all the encouragement he needed. He dragged her as close as he could with one wrist cuffed to hers and hugged her with all his strength. Her free arm wrapped around him and he knew he'd made the right choice. The only choice.

"Oh, Janey, you don't know how I've missed you." Now that he was holding her, the words raced out. "I need you so much."

She buried her face in his neck, inhaling the scent of him, loving the feel of his skin against her mouth. She kissed his ear, his jaw, his cheekbone, clinging to him, afraid she would waken and find his being here, his loving her, was only a dream. She couldn't bear to be alone again.

The door burst open and Annie rushed in. "C.J., I just saw that Chris's Jeep is—"

She came to a dead stop and gasped as she took in the sight of C.J. and Chris on the bed. C.J. gave Chris a tiny apologetic smile.

"About time you came to claim her, Chris," Annie chided. "But handcuffs?" One blond eyebrow rose suggestively.

"She did it." He pointed to C.J. and smiled wryly.

Annie's eyes widened even more. "Oh, big sister, I didn't know you had it in you."

With that she walked out, firmly closing the door behind her.

Chris shook his head. "What's she going to do now that the running's over?"

"She's decided she needs to grow up, and that she needs space from my smothering to do it."

"Ouch."

C.J. gave him a small smile. "Yeah, it did hurt, but she's right. I tend to step in and take over when I think she's done something impulsive, or what I consider foolish, and she tends to let me. She says she's going to apply to a college in Portland, Oregon."

"You know," he said slowly, "if you lived in Northfield, you'd be much closer to Portland."

C.J. felt her heart stop for a long moment as she took in the implications behind his words. Was he asking... Could he really mean... "Northfield?"

"I figure we could get married there."

"Married?" she echoed, her heart soaring.

He rattled the cuffs around their wrists. "I'm not letting you out of these until I've convinced you—"

He was offering her everything she wanted and needed. "I'm convinced. It's just that... I love you. I want to spend the rest of my life with you. I just thought I'd blown everything."

With a gentle finger, he brushed at the tiny tear that trickled down her cheek. "I should have been more understanding and less angry with you. But you were so important to me, are important to me."

His hands inched up to caress the column of her neck, his fingers wonderfully warm and erotic on C.J.'s skin. She closed her eyes, lost in sensations she would never be able to ignore, that she couldn't live without.

"The only thing left to solve is your photography," he said, his mouth against her ear, his breath warm. "There aren't a lot of big cities in this part of the country."

"I'd noticed that," she answered, barely able to concentrate on the conversation when all she wanted was for him to make love to her.

"The scenery changes, though. More than you'd think. And there's a lot of wildlife."

"I like wildlife," she said as he nibbled her ear-lobe.

"You do?" He inched closer to her on the small bed, stilling her answer with a soft kiss, the lightest brush of his lips to hers.

His mouth was warm. Tender. So incredible. Ecstasy and torture. All C.J. had ever wanted, would ever want through the many nights ahead. She drank greedily of his kiss, speared her fingers through the rich silk of his hair, ran her hand across his broad, muscled shoulders. Her softness curved to fit the hard length of him.

The perfect fit that would be hers forever.

"And I hear children photograph really well," she said on a sigh of longing.

"Children?" Chris raised his head so he could look into her eyes. "As in *our* children?"

"Chris, I love you and I want to live with you. Here. This is where you belong."

"Where we both belong," he emphasized. "And if you get restless for the big city—"

"I'm sure you could find some way to amuse me...." She grinned up at him.

That dimple on her left cheek deepened invitingly. He tightened his arm around her, pressing her closer to him as he lowered his mouth to hers. He needed tangible proof that she was his. She moaned softly, snuggling deeper into his embrace as she traced his mouth with the tip of her tongue. The fire she started so easily burned through his body.

She was his. For now. Forever. He gently lowered her onto the bed.

*   *   *   *   *

A romantic collection that
will touch your heart....

**Mother
with
Love
'93**

to

**Diana Palmer
Debbie Macomber
Judith Duncan**

As part of your annual tribute to
motherhood, join three of Silhouette's
best-loved authors as they celebrate the
joy of one of our most precious gifts—
mothers.

Available in May at your favorite retail outlet.

Only from 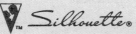 *Silhouette*®

—where passion lives.

Take 4 bestselling love stories FREE

Plus get a FREE surprise gift!

AMERICAN HERO

You have spoken! You've asked for more of our irresistible American Heroes, and now we're happy to oblige. After all, we're as in love with these men as you are! In coming months, look for these must-have guys:

In COLD, COLD HEART (IM #487) by Ann Williams, we're looking at a hero with a heart of ice. But when faced with a desperate mother and a missing child, his heart begins to melt. You'll want to be there in April to see the results!

In May we celebrate the line's tenth anniversary with one of our most-requested heroes ever: Quinn Eisley. In QUINN EISLEY'S WAR (IM #493) by Patricia Gardner Evans, this lone-wolf agent finally meets the one woman who is his perfect match.

The weather starts to heat up in June, so come deep-sea diving with us in Heather Graham Pozzessere's BETWEEN ROC AND A HARD PLACE (IM #499). Your blood will boil right along with Roc Trellyn's when he pulls in his net to find—his not-quite-ex-wife!

AMERICAN HEROES. YOU WON'T WANT TO MISS A SINGLE ONE—ONLY FROM

INTIMATE MOMENTS®
Silhouette®

IMHER04

INTIMATE MOMENTS®
Silhouette®

Silhouette Intimate Moments is proud to present:
The SISTER, SISTER duet—Two halves of a whole, two
parts of a soul.

Mary Anne Wilson's duo continues next month with
TWO AGAINST THE WORLD (IM #489). Now it's Alicia's
turn to get herself out of a dangerous bind—and into
the arms of the kindest, sexiest man she's ever seen!

If you missed the first book in the series, *Two for the Road* (IM #472), about Alicia's identical
twin sister, Alison, you can order it by sending your name, address, zip or postal code along
with a check or money order (please do not send cash) for $3.39, plus 75¢ postage and han-
dling ($1.00 in Canada), payable to Silhouette Books, to:

In the U.S.

Silhouette Books
3010 Walden Avenue
P.O. Box 1396
Buffalo, NY 14269-1396

In Canada

Silhouette Books
P.O. Box 609
Fort Erie, Ontario
L2A 5X3

Please specify book title(s) with your order.
Canadian residents add applicable federal and provincial taxes.   SISTER1